IN THE LIGHT OF DAY

Book III

The Accounts
of a Pleiadian Traveler

Nakala Akasie

Point of Light Pleiadian Publishing

All rights reserved. No part of this book may be reproduced, stored in, or introduced into a retrieval system, or transmitted in any form, or by any means (electronic, mechanical, photocopying, recording, or otherwise) without the prior written permission of the publisher.

© 2015 Nakala Akasie All rights reserved.
www.whenangelsspeaktous.com

ISBN: 978-1-942445-03-6
(e) ISBN: 978-1-942445-02-9

Library of Congress Control Number: 2015942196

Printed in the United States of America
10 9 8 7 6 5 4 3 2 1

Cover designer: Marsha Slomowitz
Typographer: Marsha Slomowitz
eBook: Marcia Breece

ALSO, BY NAKALA AKASIE
AKA JACKIE MULLINAX

When Angels Speak
The Awakening: Book One
A PLEIADIAN ENDEAVOR

Awakening: The Gift
THE ACCOUNTS OF A PLEIADIAN TRAVELER
BOOK ONE

The Sacred Contract
THE ACCOUNTS OF A PLEIADIAN TRAVELER
BOOK THREE

Soon to be released

Mirrors: Holding the Vision
THE ACCOUNTS OF A PLEIADIAN TRAVELER
BOOK FOUR

CONTENTS

PART FOUR
TO THINE OWN SELF BE TRUE

ACKNOWLEDGEMENTS

When there is Love there is Light.
Tranquil is the Presence of the Lord.

Another realm … another dream.
I am a Pleiadian traveler.
My soul seeks the wisdom of Spirit—God.
My consciousness is infinite,
always expanding—never ceasing.

INTRODUCTION

By The Akasie

We give forth great measures of Light to the World of the Physical. In our days we find joy as we assist those who traverse the Earth as they go about the endeavor of remembering to Be their true self. To recognize the God Within.

The book, *In The Light of Day* is a compilation of true experiences and channeled visions ALL for the purpose to assist the people on Earth in learning that there is always a higher purpose; a higher road. With God all things are possible. We are healers and writers. We are mystics and musicians. We are Gods and Goddesses. This is what we do. This is who we are.

PART
ONE

THIS THING CALLED LOVE

CHAPTER
ONE

The sound of my phone startled me, pulling me up from a deep sleep. My first thought was how inconsiderate for someone to call me so late at night. I swore out loud at the audacity—the nerve! Then I quickly shifted my stance as I remembered the people in my family, wondering if someone was calling me because of an accident or possibly a passing. More likely, I reasoned, someone was drunk and simply had dialed the wrong number.

I squinted at the glowing red numbers on the alarm clock trying to make sense of what it said. For a few moments everything was blurred. Then it all came into focus. The clock read 1:30 a.m. I was having trouble focusing my attention on what I was supposed to do next. Neither my mind nor my body wanted to respond to the demanding phone's ring tone.

Blindly, I reached for the phone. In the process I bumped the shade of the lamp, nearly knocking it off the table. *What could anyone possible want at this ungodly hour?*

I found the accept button on the phone and pushed it, fully expecting to hear a slurred voice on the other end calling out for a John or a Bob, but instead what I heard sent cold chills down my body. It was my brother, David's voice I heard…*but he had passed on almost fifteen years ago.* I shook myself awake, instantly going into high alert. He was saying that he wanted to meet me…to talk to me about something concerning Mom and Dad. My mind refused to process what I was hearing. I couldn't think. Is this some sort of practical joke? Like nothing was out of the ordinary, the voice on the other end kept talking, saying tomorrow about 11:00 a.m. would work for him. Then he paused and I heard him take a deep breath. I hadn't said anything except for hello in the entire conversation. *Was this for real? What should I say? What should I do?* Then working to sort out what was happening, I heard myself ask, "David is that you?"

He laughed as if I had said something absurd and replied, "Of Course it is me. Do you have another brother I don't know about? Who else would it be?" I stammered, my words broken, "But…you died. You died…how can you possibly be speaking to me now…now on this phone?" David didn't pause to think about what I had asked but responded in a clear, sure voice, "I am not dead!"

Sounding entirely annoyed, he said, "Look, I want to make this perfectly clear. I am quite able to communicate with you. How could I possibly be dead?" I heard myself say, "Wait," trying to clear my mind. I thought I must be dreaming; or worse, maybe I was hallucinating.

Then I heard David speaking again, "You are not dreaming, and no you are not hallucinating." "Wait…how?... I didn't say that out loud…how did you know what I was thinking?"

"You know quite well what I am talking about—telepathic communications." In his voice I heard deep sense of frustration but he kept at it. "You use this type of communication every day with your guides and the angels. Don't you? Why are you questioning this?" I didn't answer him. He was correct, there was no need.

Fifteen years ago, David had died from an overdose—a mixture of some sort of pills—uppers, downers—I don't know. David's death certificate arbitrarily stated that the cause of death was a heart attack. Well, that would do it alright—taking a handful of pills, that is, sending the heart into overdrive by giving it mixed signals—basically confusing it until it shut down entirely. I had been outraged with my brother for being so stupid—his actions. I mean really? David cut in interrupting my thoughts. "Look," he said out loud, "I know what I did and how it upset the family." I was shocked by his choice of nullifying words. "*Upset the family?*"

"You have got to be kidding me here, I said in a harsh tone. 'Upset the family?' More like threw everyone into a tailspin." I heard the anger in my voice. I was agitated, unable to hide my feelings any longer. Again he interrupted me and said, "This is not the time to get into what I did or didn't do. I am *asking* you to meet me and talk to me about Mom and Dad."

Perplexed and disillusioned, my emotions exploded, taking me down a path of self-righteous indignation. I took the straight reality of it all and practically yelled, "Look, I can't meet you! You are dead!" I shook my head working to assess my sanity then I punched the off button and slammed the phone down hard on the night table only to have it begin playing its infuriating ringtone once again. I hesitated before I picked up the phone again. This time I looked closely at the numbers as they did a digital dance across the screen before I pushed the accept button. It read 316-532-9804. Wait…isn't that my sister-in-laws number? *What?* I froze. Time seemed to stand still. I felt weak—sick. I didn't look at the number from the previous call. I felt a ripple of fear run through my body—cold and unwelcome. Not knowing what to do, I got out of bed and began to pace for what seemed like an eternity. I felt utterly terrified and alone. *Whose voice would I hear on the other end this time?*

Why was I afraid? I had channeled unseen spirits: guides, masters, angels and even disembodied spirits (those who have passed on), for years. I knew that when they are highly motivated to contact someone they most certainly can and *will* find a way to do it! But to hear my very own brother's voice like that shook me to the very core of my being. *How can a disembodied spirit call someone up on the phone and speak to them?*

I was caught in a spell of some sort as the ringtone continued to play on my phone. Mentally, I wished—prayed—for it to stop, for my recorder to pick up, but it didn't. *Do I dare answer the phone?* Before I could stop myself I pushed the accept button. "Hello?" I squeezed my eyes shut hoping that this action somehow would shield me—protect me from hearing, feeling…anything.

It was him again—my brother—I heard his voice clear solid—distinctly commanding me, "Do not hang up." Again, he repeated his request.

"I want to talk to you about Mom and Dad. I have important information." Without waiting for my response he continued, "Meet me at the Old Railroad Depot in Newton at 11:00 in the morning. Be on time." Not waiting for my reply he abruptly disconnected.

Petrified, I stood there, looking at the phone in my hand, half expecting the thing to explain what just happened. But it lay on my hand motionless—dead just like my brother was…

Not knowing how to figure out what had just occurred I took a long cleansing breath and just stood there for what seemed like several minutes. Then I glanced at the digital clock and saw that a mere ten minutes had passed, but my entire life had taken a hundred and eighty degree turn. *Newton? That is just thirty minutes from where I live. I wondered if what he might say would give me some clarity on my current situation.*

My brother? Not dead? Able to call me on the phone, no less, and talk to me? I had seen his body—lifeless—prostrate in that coffin that day. I know he had passed from his physical body. I shook my head in defiance—utter disbelief. This was impossible. I thought that I might have gone crazy. "God help me please," I whispered.

I figured there would be no more sleeping tonight so I decided to take a shower to help ease the anxiety. What I *really* needed was a week of deep sleep. Now I wondered if I would even be able to rest after this.

The hot water calmed me somewhat and as soon as I hit the pillow I was out.

CHAPTER
TWO

Morning came early, too early, in my opinion. I did not want to face the day. I did not want to think about what had happened in the middle of the night. I mean seriously, it had to be a bad dream. *A super bad dream. Right?*

But I still looked at the call log on my phone for proof…that I wasn't crazy. "Oh God," I muttered, it was still there…the number.

Eleven o'clock was what David had told me. There was not much time to figure out what I was going to do. David had told me to meet him at the Old Train Depot which was thirty minutes away. I just couldn't seem to wrap my mind around what I was told to do. Why was this so difficult? I worked with the unseen every single day! But this particular time I was perplexed. This just shouldn't be so difficult.

Suddenly, Nathanal my spiritual guide reminded me that there is so much out there that I was unfamiliar with and didn't understand yet. Nathanal told me, "Be with it. Remember you are here for the journey. Have an open mind through this and see what happens."

So, I did just that. I made sure I was in front of the depot at 11:00 sharp just as David had instructed.

Leading up to the front entrance of the Old Train Depot, there was an extra-wide walk edged with a thick curved half-wall of brick. It was the correct height for people to sit down on to wait for whatever reason. I made a mental note that I had a great view of who came and went.

The depot had been a hot spot back during World War II and now it was a station for Amtrak Railroad Passenger Corporation. I saw that a popular restaurant shared the expansive red brick building as well.

Just as I sat down on the brick wall, I pulled out my cell phone to check the time. It read 10:54. Ah, I still had a few minutes to wait.

During the twenty-four mile drive, I had felt the apprehension in the pit of my stomach grow. No amount of breathing, praying or talking to myself or God during the drive had eased the tension.

I was contemplating on walking back to my car, getting in it and heading back home when I saw a man on the west end of the parking lot walking toward me. As he neared, his profile came into view, then the details—his dark brown hair pulled back in a ponytail, his full mustache. He wore a blue plaid flannel shirt, the buttons pulled tight over his bulging stomach, faded blue jeans, and those awful clunky work boots. His face came into view and I knew…In silence I laughed. The way he carried himself and dressed, I always thought that he had come straight from an earlier era, the one when the men were riding horses across the western plains in search of wealth and women.

That is when I began to pray: Dear God, in heaven, what are you do-ing to me? I whispered under my breath to Nathanal to please steady me because I really thought I might be sick— real soon.

I shifted my body a little and grabbed the edges of the jagged brick wall to hold on to for support. As David walked closer, I could tell he saw me and knew who I was. Our eyes met. Goose bumps covered my body.

From way back, I never really liked my brother—I never trusted him. And this? This *little* incident was certainly no exception. This felt like he was playing a very cruel joke on me to show up like this so many years after he had passed.

I swallowed hard and shook my head again to try to clear my doubt—my fear. It wasn't working. The closer he got the more afraid I became, and I realized I didn't want to do this! I didn't care what information he had about Mom and Dad.

I felt stuck—trapped—powerless—unable to make myself stand up and walk away. He was twenty feet away and fast approaching. Expertly, I scanned his features for any detail to prove that what I was seeing wasn't real, that this wasn't him. I looked at his face again and saw his eyes. He had a lazy eye as a boy that had remained through adulthood. Yup, it was still there. I sucked in a breath.

The circumstances surrounding David's death came flooding back in my mind again. He had had such a volatile life. Since an early age my brother had had countless run-ins with the law and was known to do drugs and drank more than a fair amount of alcohol. I felt a heaviness as the memories collected and pooled. Then I shook my head and chuckled to myself as the memory of being told that my brother had gotten into a brawl with the Chief of Police in our small town…how it had ended by the Chief's nose being broken and my brother being cuffed and jailed. I had been embarrassed and ashamed to be in the same family.

However, a few months before David's passing we saw a change in his outlook on life. David had been invited to go on a mission trip to Nicaragua. To my amazement he had gone!

I remember how persuasive my mother sounded when she talked about David like she had wanted to convince me—or possibly she had been working to convince herself—that he was doing better. When she spoke of David like that I always felt a miniscule thread of hope that *this* time he might get his life under control.

The plan had been to travel to Nicaragua for three weeks. They had gone to reroof homes for the poor with metal sheeting. When he came home he had said that they slept on the roofs to get a breeze, if there had been one that is. He had said that the days were sweltering and the nights were about as bad. The men on the trip had not really been able to get a good night's rest. He returned home twenty pounds lighter, looking tired but robust and happier than he had in years.

After that trip, there had been days when he had been sober and we had been able to talk with him. Our hopes had finally been lifted only to come crashing down— hard, again! It had felt like, *this time,* he had been going to win.

David had left four young children and a wife behind. I didn't think I could ever forgive him. I didn't want to. What he had done seemed unjustifiable and downright inexcusable—mean.

David had gone off somewhere and parked his truck and died. When he didn't come home that night his wife had waited until the next morning to call the police. His one-year-old daughter, not old enough to conceive that her daddy would never come home, for months had cried for her daddy.

Now the children are grown. The last one is almost out of school. Why on earth would I want to talk to this man now after all of these years? I shook my head in defiance, finding the anger to rise from my seat and walk away. Instead, I found myself face to face with my brother. Yup, this was him. There was no doubt.

I saw the questions in his eyes. He had read my intention. He knew how I felt, all right. With his hands he made a motion for me to sit. He did not offer me his hand nor did he attempt to give me he a hug. There were no apologies spoken nor did he ask for my forgiveness.

Stunned…still angry, I hesitated before I slowly sat back down on the cool brick wall.

I kept my eyes focused on the sight before me. My very own brother, David, who had been laid out flat—inanimate at his own funeral—to never again rise—who I believed to be long gone from this world was now standing erect before me, creating a shadow of sorts shielding me from the sun's rays. I wanted to reach out and feel the soft texture of his shirt. However, something deep inside me cautioned me that perhaps this wasn't a smart thing to do. I wanted to feel the realness of this person. But I did not.

I did not speak to him. I merely waited for him to take the initiative. I saw him stand there for many moments looking down at me. I looked in his eyes and saw an ache, a raw vulnerability there. *Was it sadness that I saw?*

Finally, David sat down beside me at an angle so he could see me as he spoke. Lightly, his knee touched mine and I felt an electric shock travel up my body and overtake my senses. Quickly, I moved back a few inches away from him as I looked up into his eyes and asked, "What the heck?" He moved his hands as if to wipe away the infraction as he said, "I am sorry. It is a hazard of sorts."

No other explanation was offered and I did not ask.

David took a deep breath and I knew he was about to have his say. "What I did so many years ago, I did to escape the pain I felt." With his words, he had captured my attention and I let him continue without interruption. "I was constantly tormented by severe highs and lows that I did not understand. I could not control them no matter how hard I tried and no matter what I did. The drugs, the alcohol, had been a way to escape—to try to control those swings, those feelings. I hated myself, my life. I loved my family my children and by doing the things I did knew I was hurting my family. I knew all of this and I knew that leaving them behind like I did would hurt them, as well. But I figured that they would be better off without me."

I was shocked by his unexpected revelation and asked, "You mean you did this—killed yourself on purpose? I always thought it was an accident. I mean, I always knew that sooner or later you would end up hurting yourself really bad or killing yourself, but to do it on purpose?" I shook my head not understanding the full implications of his words.

He waved his hands as if to somehow calm me and said, "No, I didn't decide that day to kill myself. It just happened because I wanted to die. But, that is not the reason I am here…to explain my actions so long ago."

He paused to gather his words before he continued, "I am here on a mission of sorts. I know you work with the hierarchy—the angels—your guides. I know that you talk to them; they guide you and you write together. I also know that since I left you have been the sole caregiver for Mom and Dad. It was *never* my intention to leave you hanging."

David didn't wait for me to counter, "From my vantage point, as it is now, I have absolute clarity of my actions during that time—the impact I had on *everyone's* lives. I have watched my children grow up without me. I have watched my wife struggle with raising the children, her depression— her drinking and her thoughts of wanting to end it all—to join me."

He saw my expression and knew I had questions, but he did not wait for me to voice them. Instead, with conviction, he continued on, his voice etched in sorrow, "Oh, yes, the pain ran *that* deep. Now, three of my children are grown and my eldest son has a family of his own. Time has a way of easing the pain somewhat."

He stopped voicing his recollections and looked up deeply into my eyes. "Nakala? That is what they call you now, right? You think that once a person ends their physical existence that the person stops caring?"

Frustrated and angry, I countered, "They have to care in the first place, you know! Why did you call me? What is it you want to talk to me about?" The venom had surfaced in fullness. I was enraged and had been for my entire life at this person for his inconsiderate and vicious ways. He had seemed to hate everyone in his path and I had been one of his *lucky* beneficiaries.

Then I saw it—the expression on his face, the shame, the embarrassment. I saw that he was truly sorry he had treated me the way he had. *Was he here to make amends?*

"Look," he began, "I know I was a terrible brother—I was a terrible person! But that is not why I am here. I am not here to talk about how awful I was until the day I took those pills. I came because of Mom and Dad. They are getting up there, in age. Their bodies, both of them, are weak and their minds are failing them." His voice and words were becoming stronger, gaining speed—momentum. "I know you do what you can for them. I know Dad is in a nursing home. I know Mom married that guy—the one we all warned her about." He was shaking his head now and chuckled under his breath. Then he took a deep breath and sighed, "I have watched all of you. I have stood beside you countless times without your knowing I was there. I wanted to talk to you to tell you…to make you understand. But, I could not. Then one day Nathanal, yes Nathanal, your guide, came to me and said it is your sister, Nakala, I serve. It is she whom I assist. In assisting her, I want to offer you something unique, something that can be quite useful that will benefit the entire family.

"Nathanal I know, as he is the one who is usually standing beside you. He protects you—loves you. Usually, he acknowledges my presence but doesn't usually engage in any sort of communication with me."

David had my full attention then. The words 'that will benefit the entire family' had stirred something deep in me and I wanted to hear his proposal. So I listened to him and listened closely.

David continued his narrative, "that one day, Nathanal had told me that I could ask for assistance to make things right if I wanted to. He knew I did! So I said yes, I wanted to ask, but I had wondered if it wasn't too late to fix things. I mean my kids are grown. Mom and Dad were almost ready to make their transitions. You had moved on away from the family, as well. The family has grown distant with one another almost like the family never existed in the first place. Nathanal assured me that at some point healing must occur and it would be best to begin right now. He is the one who arranged for me to meet someone who seemed to know everything about our family and I began to work with him."

I cleared my throat. In a small voice, I asked, "Who was it David? Who worked with you?"

David's answer stunned me, "Babaró." Instantly hot tears sprang to my eyes as I thought of all the times Babaró had counseled me. Just as I thought of Babaró I felt a deep love wash over me. I had to smile. I had to laugh.

It was then the memory surfaced of another time Babaró had pulled something of this nature on me.

It had been a Saturday. I could see the sun streaming through the window on a summer afternoon, shortly after my divorce had been finalized, when I received a phone call on my cell phone.

I had been in the kitchen as I listened to a man on the other end of the line identify himself as Dr. Phil. I heard a pronounced southern twang in his voice, but being skeptical, I had asked again, "Who's calling?" The man repeated his introduction, "This is Dr. Phil."

In dismay, I shook my head thinking this couldn't be true. For the third time, I asked, "No, really. Who *IS* this?" This time he had sounded a bit irritated as he repeated, "This is Dr. Phil."

As this man, *Dr. Phil,* spoke, I noticed he didn't mince words. The way he spoke, it seemed to me that he was egotistical, a know-it-all to the extent of being very obnoxious.

Carefully, I listened to this man's voice as I recalled how Dr. Phil spoke on his TV show. I did not believe it was *really Dr. Phil.*

Dr. Phil began a series of questions concerning my family. They were all related to my relationships—how I felt toward these people—my mother, daughter and so on. He asked if I held resentment or anger, to describe my relationship with them.

Logically, I knew that I could hang up on this guy at any time, but for some reason, I had chosen not to. I had been held captivated like what was happening was a game of some sort.

Throughout the conversation, I had felt like this guy, whoever he was, sure had balls to call me up and ask me these personal questions. After all I did *not* ask him to intrude in my life this way.

At any rate, I stayed with his questions the best I could. Then *Dr. Phil* said, out of the blue. "You are divorced." My voice had stuck in my throat for a moment. A little voice said he could be guessing. The stats were staggering at the number of divorced couples these days. The percentage might be viewed as devastating.

I revealed that I was getting one. *Dr. Phil* then began to counsel me. "You will never heal from this until you look him in the eyes and tell him how you truly feel. Never!"

My mouth dropped open as he cleverly had changed the subject. He asked, "Are you taking any drugs?" At that point I was offended and sarcastically answered, "No, but I take vitamins! Would you like to know which ones?"

As if he were truly interested, without missing a beat, *Dr. Phil* had answered, "Yes, I would." I thought to myself, how odd, and then proceeded to give him a rundown of my regimen. I was angry. He had crossed the line. This information was none of his business. *None of it was his business!*

When I had finished, abruptly *Dr. Phil* stated, "Got to go." "What?" I asked not believing that he was about to hang up—that our little game of wit was about to be end. Again, he repeated, "Got to go," Not waiting for me to reply, he disconnected.

It had all been surreal—inconceivable—incredible. I had stood there for several minutes reviewing the entire conversation in total suspicion, not knowing what the true purpose of the phone call had been.

✳ ✳ ✳

After I had spent some time thinking and reassessing what had occurred, I looked at the phone log to see if I could figure out anything from that. The area code was not from Kansas so I looked it up on the Internet and saw that it was from California. Swiftly, I decided to call my friend and neighbor, Suzan, and tell her what had happened. Her response was shock. "How could you give out information to a total stranger like that?" "Well," I explained, "I didn't give out anything of a financial sort—nothing that would reveal my identity."

Then Suzan gave me a couple of ideas. "Call the number back and see what happens and do a search on the Internet. See if you can get his phone number or as least write him on his website for him to contact you."

I did just what she had advised me. Funny, the number that *Dr. Phil* had called me from was now, suddenly, out of service. Then I found his website and wrote him a letter. Nothing panned out. My skepticism was quickly growing into suspicion. Either someone had just pulled an A-One prank on me or one of my guides had been responsible. But I questioned…how could a guide make a phone call or talk on the phone? They are not of the physical realm.

Earlier when I had first begun to work with my guides, they would make all sorts of racket and there were times that I had heard voices outside of myself that I knew to be my guides. *Who was the man who had called me?*

* * *

As the weekend proceeded, I relayed the story to a couple of other friends. One of them, John, had become excited and offered, "Oh, I'll tell you what happened to me."

I had listened intently, hoping to get a clue as to the real identity of the person who called himself *Dr. Phil.*

John had been a railroad man and had just been called to work, "I was at the motel and had been there for about five hours. Earlier I had been reading an angel book and wanted to find out the name of my angel, so I said, "I'd really like to know what your name is. Please let me know." I was really tired so I lay down I went to sleep. Soon thereafter I heard the phone ring. I had been in a deep sleep and wasn't on top of my game, when I answered the phone. I said, 'Hello.' On the other end I heard a voice say, 'Seneca.'

"I had asked, 'What?' 'Seneca.' I just couldn't figure out what it was about so asked, 'Are you looking for Sean who is on my crew?' There was no answer…nothing." John went on to say, "I hung up the phone and thought about it. I wanted to get to the bottom of it. Since this was still in the switchboard days, I called the switchboard up and asked if they had patched any calls to my room. The answer was, 'no.'"

Later John had remembered his request that he had made to his guardian angel. The more he had thought about it the more intrigued he had become. There had never been another explanation offered to John concerning his telephone call. However, he believed that his guardian angel had made the call.

At that point, I was fully enmeshed in why someone had wanted to make the Dr. Phil phone call to me and why! I decided then to ask my guides about it. To me, it was obvious that the person was not the Dr. Phil who had the TV show.

The very next day I had driven to the big city where my soon to be ex-husband worked. Remembering the message I received about healing I decided, off the cuff, to call him up to ask him to lunch. Normally, one, he would never pick up the phone; two, he would never be available.

I had been married for thirty-five years to this man and this was his pattern. This time he picked up and said he was available at that moment. I was five minutes away so we agreed to meet. I was astonished at my good fortune. We met and I explained to him that I felt we needed to really talk in order to heal from our divorce—the circumstances concerning it. (Who doesn't?) We were able to have a really great conversation. I told him that I wanted him to be happy. (It was my way of freeing him.) I felt like we were not growing as individuals. A week later, he called me to tell me he was getting married. Ironic…

Throughout this ordeal, it became evident that the same guide, Babaró, who had talked to my brother had also taken on the persona of *Dr. Phil* and made that phone call. Had it been to get me to look at my relationships? I mean really look, or perhaps it was a way to ease me into the announcement of the upcoming nuptials? Maybe it had been both reasons.

The guides were good all right. I had seen first-hand how the high masters and guides plotted and planned to help me in the realization that my very own thoughts create my reality. They had (and still do) a direct impact on everything: my feelings, my health, my work, my relationships—every single aspect of my life has been created by what I think and how I feel.

So it had begun with the guides training me to realize what and when I was creating certain thoughts that were negative. Of course, everything is interconnected and not so simple. But even so, my guides had stayed the course, not ever giving up on me. Now I see they were working with my family members as well; even the ones who were no longer living in a physical body to assist us in healing long past traumas and self-imposed false beliefs.

* * *

I turned and gave David a smile as I said, "I am beginning to understand that it is fully possible and also time to heal past hurts. But, what is this thing about Mom and Dad?" In turn, he smiled, and I felt this immense burden lift from the both of us as he said, "what is done is done. We can't go back to change things we have done no matter how much we would like to."

It was then that I knew all was forgiven—forgotten. There was no more anger, no more resentment and most of all there was no more fear. I was at peace.

* * *

In the distance, I had heard the train making its way toward us, and then I heard its loud whistle. I looked around and saw the bustle of activity, the movement before me. Dozens of people were going here and there: an old man walking his poodle, a young couple out for some fresh air, a new mother pushing her baby in a stroller.

Across the street, I watched children playing in the well-manicured city park. The pink azaleas were in full bloom and so beautiful! The depot itself was teaming with visitors. Some of the people were heading inside for tickets or maybe lunch.

With a jolt, I realized that David was no longer sitting beside me. He had gone, vanished. Perhaps he had never been there in the first place— what I had experienced was possibly no more than a vision, a dream. How strange all of it had been.

There I sat at a train station in Newton because of the prompting of a phone call. At this moment nothing seemed to matter or be more important than to just sit and watch the people go about their daily activities.

CHAPTER
THREE

After the drive home from Newton, I immersed myself in working on a watercolor painting. I had needed an activity that was relaxing—that I could easily lose myself in. During the entire drive, I had been in a mental fog. Periods of time were missing. I had replayed the scene at the train depot over and over, picking apart every detail, every word.

To believe that what I experienced had been real—whether David, my brother, had indeed come to talk to me or it had been just a vision of some sort that my guides had orchestrated on my behalf—had been difficult for me to get past. I knew they could do that sort of thing if they chose to—if they wanted to.

I knew the purpose for the meeting with David was for healing limiting core beliefs and past hurts. Still, my mind whirled with questions. How did a person who had stepped out of the third dimension (the world of the physical) with the action of so-called death suddenly have the ability to waltz back into it in the same physical body without going through the process of reincarnation? He had looked like anyone else in that parking lot…and yet I remember distinctly avoiding any sort of touch between the two of us. I had felt intuitively it might not be a wise thing. In my opinion, the entire incident had been very strange.

On the way home, I had asked Nathanal what he knew about the episode and his response had been, "Nakala, it would be better if you talk to Babaró or Samuel Paul about it."

Past experience told me of course it would be better to talk to one of the masters who work with me. On the other hand, in the past, it seemed that I had to wait until one of the masters had been ready to make the initiative to reveal certain information to me. Understanding that the answers I sought were multifaceted, I decided to let it go. I could easily wait until everything aligned for me to receive the information.

Instead, I turned my attention to the watercolor painting I was working on. The dramatic colors of ocean life excited me in a way that spurred me on. The vivid turquoises and greens stirred my senses taking me deeper into the blue sea. Frankly, the colors made me want to go scuba diving with the dolphins, fish and sea creatures. Up close, I wanted to examine the sea world and explore unknown territories. In the painting, I had incorporated different shades peaches, corals, yellows and oranges in the plant life; and the whole effect, I felt, was rather pleasing.

Time passed quickly, and soon I had forgotten the "scene" earlier that morning.

It was my habit every evening to meditate before bed. Tonight was no exception. As soon as I had gotten comfortable, I began to breathe deeply and empty my mind of all the clutter of the day. I was so calm that when I heard someone talking to me, I was easily able to ignore them.

It had been Samuel Paul who had spoken my name. It sounded like a faraway breeze that beckoned me. I waited to respond, not wanting to break away from the moment of silence. I heard him again gently coaxing me back into a place where I could—would communicate. "Nakala, I have words for you just now. Please come to me." This time, I didn't hesitate to answer him as he had broken through some sort of barrier.

"Nakala, as you know everything you experience is multifaceted. At this time, I'd like to share a bit of why your brother came to visit you today." Samuel Paul had spiked my interest. "Yes," I responded, "Why was David permitted to visit me like he was?"

"Yes," Samuel Paul said, "David was allowed to visit you in the physical reality which is something that is not ordinarily granted. We, the Telbar, (The Telbar is the group of beings dedicated to assisting my ascension.) decided to accelerate your healing (not only yours but also of the entire family rippling outward into the nations and beyond), by promoting the communications between you and your brother. He, David, was approached by Babaró and two other members of our group with the idea that the two of you would get together and talk about your feelings. We used the idea of his wanting to speak to you concerning your parents to entice you to meet him. Of course, you saw plainly that it wasn't your parents that he really was to discuss although it would be beneficial for you both to discuss them during your next meeting.

"Instead, of speaking to you on matters concerning your parents, it was the emotional trauma of David's untimely passing that was to be reviewed first."

At this point, all I wanted to do was to get Samuel Paul to stop talking about David's passing! I saw myself waving my hands in front of me in a gesture of desperation to catch his attention. Then I began to speak over Samuel Paul's voice. "Stop…wait…I don't want to go any further with this right now. Let this—what you have said—sink in before you go any further, please."

A part of me felt I had been deceived—tricked even, in order to get me to meet with David. I was about to go into a long list of why I felt mislead, but I didn't finish my thought. I knew better than to get into the game of blaming anyone.

Through this experience I had been given grace—released old energy, a block that had haunted me for many years. For that I was totally grateful.

Quickly, my thoughts shifted back to the cryptic statement Samuel Paul had made earlier, 'the next meeting', and the implications of what that might entail.

I had to laugh. These guides—the masters whom I work with—had done it again. They had taken a painful issue in my life which I had not worked through, and with it they had created a real-life scenario to assist me in realizing that I had created something of substance, that had been, in its own time, bit by bit, gnawing away at me. Sometimes things have a way of just waiting—simmering slowly until someone decides to add a bit of fuel to the fire.

PART
TWO

COMING HOME

CHAPTER

FOUR

The day began in a slow monotonous fashion. My plan was to go shopping but for some reason I was distracted and kept inventing more tasks to do, ultimately delaying my departure.

Nathanal had been proposing an impromptu trip north into Oregon before the cold set in for good. I had argued with him saying that I didn't want to go—that I just wanted to stay home and rest. In turn, doing his best to persuade me, he countered, "It will be months before you have another opportunity like this to get out and do some sight-seeing. You are here to enjoy yourself and experience life! So let's do it!"

I hesitated before answering. I felt drained, on more than one level, from the previous months of constant travel. This year alone, I had traveled to Prescott, Arizona for over a month, then to Brazil. After that I traveled to Mt. Shasta, California.

It had been then, during my visit to Mt. Shasta, when I had heard Sakeem say, "It is time to come home." I had been gazing at the glorious mountain, Shasta, when I had heard the message and knew that what I heard could not be ignored. Six months later, I had traveled across the country with my car loaded with my personal items to return to that beautiful place that I now call home.

I had been in California only a few weeks, just getting my feet wet, when I found my new home. The paper-work had been completed, I had moved in; but my furniture had not shipped yet. It would be at least two more weeks of *camping out* before my truck arrived.

Nathanal was correct that I should seize the moment and just go! But I had been on the road for such a long time…

I wanted…no I thought I *needed* some down time. However, I recognized the wisdom in what Nathanal suggested, so I finally accepted his offer and said, "Yes."

Once my mind was made up, I quickly loaded my car with several drinking bottles of fresh water that I had collected from the Sacramento headwaters at the Mt. Shasta City Park and anything else I thought I might need for an overnight trip.

The plan was to drive to Klamath Falls, Oregon. Immediately, I found that I had become easily excited to be on the road again with no real agenda to follow—I felt free!

The drive was rather quiet—nothing to report that was unusual or exciting. Everywhere, I looked the land was parched brown. California was going through a severe drought. Along my journey there were areas where the forest fires had made their mark. Some of the trees had had their trunks scorched. Seeing that some of the tops of the trees remained green eased some of my feelings of grief. I wondered if the trees had felt the hot flames cruelly lick at their trunks, scorching the bark that protected the tender layers of fiber inside.

Once I crossed the California border going into Oregon, the scenery drastically changed. The land looked lush; the rivers and lakes overflowing with water. Directly on both sides of the highway there were canals. As I drove further north I had noticed what I thought to be white posts as they were perfectly motionless and were evenly spaced every twenty feet or so. As I looked a little closer I saw the white posts were actually Egrets perched for their mid-day catch.

A few miles further the highway crossed a river and there huddled on the sandbar were hundreds of white pelicans. I wanted to get a picture so I pulled into the area by the bridge and jumped out of my car.

As I crossed the highway the wind violently whipped at my hair and clothes. Since I was from Kansas, seeing Pelicans nestled on a sand bar was out of the ordinary. I felt grateful that Nathanal had been so insistent to do something spontaneous for a change.

CHAPTER
FIVE

The further north I had traveled the lighter I felt. I was reminded of who I was, a Pleiadian traveler. A ripple of happiness ran deeply through my body and my heart expanded.

Suddenly, I heard one of my guides, Sakeem, begin to speak to me in a voice that left no question. Sakeem wanted to make an important point. I listened closely. "Nakala, darling, you are in a land of abundance. Look about you. The trees, they stand by the millions; like manned towers they are ever watchful. The waterways, all, are full. The birds that flock in great numbers are a sign of promise—all are flourishing. All seems to be in harmony in this place."

However, I was, at the time, unable to shake the image of the barren wasteland I had just driven through. Simply the vision was too fresh. I had judged it all, and to me it was issue of complete polarity. I wasn't yet able to fathom why this would be: the California landscape, in places had been barren, brown, and brittle, unable to support wildlife while Oregon's had been the land of plenty, lush, green; its waterways were full to overflowing, teaming with waterfowl.

I felt a raw ache that was akin to despair and vulnerability. *Why was nature in California forced to suffer?*

The landscape of the burned trees and the dry soil had deeply etched itself in my mind taking predominance over the beauty before me. I countered, "Yes, but in California, the fires left trees scarred for life and others dead. What about that is in harmony?" Immediately, I knew my statement had been negative in nature and felt a pang of regret.

"Ah, Nakala," Sakeem offered, "let me broaden your scope of vision. Whenever there is a mass exodus—or cataclysm of sorts—when God's creation is released from this third dimension, there is much rejoicing that takes place. Think on the life forms that are affected, from the tiniest microbe to the largest tree—perhaps there were people and animals who were released from their physical forms as well. Perhaps some of these beings attained a level of awareness or skill during their service on the Earth plane and were ready to graduate—to move on to a higher level of mastery. Look at it as part of the cycle of life; and for these beings, whatever form they had taken, through their release or liberation they had been given a new opportunity.

"Ah, Nakala, let me remind you that there is always more than one benefit to any action. I am not finished with what I have to show you." As I waited for Sakeem to resume his teaching, I remembered how Sakeem had first come to me a year earlier. I had just returned to Kansas, settling in from my two-week stay in Brazil at the John of God compound. I had been lying face down on a massage table in Dr. Jonah's office receiving a Flow treatment.

Sakeem, to me, had seemed unsure of himself as he introduced himself to me, and next asked if he might begin to work with me. However, now I see that it wasn't that he was unsure of himself; he just didn't want to barge in during my session. Immediately, I had asked my guides if what Sakeem asked were for my highest good and if I should accept. Their response was a quick and sure, "Yes."

Their response had come so swiftly that I had to deduce that they had been expecting my question. I wondered what they all were planning. I had repeated the name, Sakeem, over and over in my mind, thinking it unusual.

Before I could respond to Sakeem's request though, Dr. Jonah, with his usual vigor, happily proclaimed that I was good to go. With that, Sakeem's request had been temporarily placed aside...until he came to me again the following week during my next session with Dr. Jonah. This time, I accepted Sakeem's offer. It was later that Sakeem had disclosed that his station had been Telos. He collaborated with the people there in the efforts to reach the mainstream people on the surface of the Earth.

Suddenly, I heard Sakeem say my name, bringing me back from my reverie. "Nakala, you have been told that these cataclysmic events are the result of collective thoughts created by the mass consciousness. This is truth. But, what you haven't been told is with every event that tears down, the result is a grand opportunity, as a collective, to rebuild something—something even better.

"The fires, I speak of them. The trees when turned to ash, given the correct set of circumstances will create carbon-rich minerals that will encourage or have a positive effect on new growth.

"I put it another way. When you want to remodel—say a bathroom, depending on the level of renovating intended, do you not have to first tear down and remove the old before you can rebuild and make better? The same goes with revivifying forests. Honey, I hear your objections. In a perfect world death and decay does not exist. But since you are in a dense third dimensional world, that for now, in your eyes, is not perfect, there must be cycles to transition, to transform, to renew in order to evolve and raise the vibration. This is all in conjunction with your process to move higher—expanding your level of consciousness.

"So now, I ask you, when you look upon an area that has been wiped-out, so to speak, remember my words as this that you are viewing is merely a step in the transition—the process of rebirth. Look at it as a great gift from our Supreme Creator to restore the culminated energies."

I was beginning to process why we have *these* events, but Sakeem felt I should receive further explanation. "I have another example, as I wish not to become redundant. Since you are an artist this comparison will most definitely resonate with you.

"Look at the forest as if it were a painted canvas. The oils used were heavily laden with rich pigments and applied to the canvas in such a fashion to uplift and please the artist/observer. Over the years, the paints dried out, discolored and faded; they grew brittle from the process of oxidation. Ultimately, the paints cracked and began to flake off.

"After a time, it had become evident that the painting had gone beyond the point of being worthwhile of being repaired. Perhaps it was impossible to repair it well enough to restore it to its pristine order. Perhaps it was for the highest good to start over with a clean canvas.

"The Earth is the canvas, the forest is the painting—God's creation. When energy becomes old, and has deteriorated beyond repair it is time to start anew." I saw his point of view but still felt like there was so much life that had been needlessly taken.

Sakeem heard my thought and again reminded me, "Nakala, for the present time, please understand that you are stationed on this Earth and you, as well as all other life-forms, experience cycles: conception, gestation, birth, all the phases of growth into adulthood when you yourself are able to create life. Then as you age you enter the golden years and then the body is discarded."

Suddenly, I heard, Sakeem say, "That is enough of that. It is time to move on. You see clearly, there is a season for everything.

"I'd like to discuss another topic if you don't mind." I shrugged my shoulders and said, "Sure, why not?"

"There is the matter of your brother, David. We have not spoken of this one for some time. Do you realize what date it is?" I hadn't thought about it at all as I am not one to constantly be looking at the calendar for so-called important dates. I answered politely, "Yes, I know it is September, my son's and my granddaughter's birthdays."

Pausing, I went deeper to retrieve other important dates for September. As I waited for Sakeem to get on with his teaching I was careful not to reveal my feelings. I answered, "It is also the anniversary of the falling of the Twin Towers and yes, the anniversary of my brother's passing."

To me it seemed like forever and then it seemed like just yesterday as the images of us gathered at my brother's home after the announcement of his death had remained in graphic detail—fixed in my memory.

Sakeem was not going to let me off the hook. Yet he refrained from going forward with his teaching. I felt his energy pouring into me to ease what I was feeling when he said, "I realize that you do not wish to revisit his passing. In your mind it is finished—done and there is no going back. To talk about it, to you, seems senseless."

I had to admit that I didn't want to talk about David or the family, but I couldn't completely agree with Sakeem's assessment of how I felt.

Intellectually, I knew that there still had to be underlying currents of emotion concerning David or I wouldn't be getting up from the computer to get this or that in order to put off writing.

I knew it was best to do this thing, even though I didn't really know what it was we were doing. I began by saying, "Sakeem, I feel vulnerable, like I am wounded animal lying exposed—vulnerable in the wilderness for something to finish me off. I want to heal this thing and get on with my life." His next words surprised me. "What I have to say may sting somewhat."

My eyebrows furrowed as I considered his words, *"Sting"? Why on earth would anything Sakeem have to say sting?* Nothing was making sense and I felt a surge of dread of what he was about to reveal.

Then Sakeem made his move much like a seasoned chess player who has thought over his choices—his next critical move—very carefully, saying, "What if I took the liberty and said to you that you feel a deep sense of responsibility for your brother's passing." I was dumbfounded. *Where was he going with this? Me? Responsible? Like maybe it was my fault?* My mind went empty—blank, like I had entered an incredible void of nothingness and everything at the same time. The polarity of the situation had canceled out all thought! I felt alone, afraid. Then, suddenly, I broke through the emptiness, retrieving my thoughts and again I was able to speak. "No, I am not at fault. How can I be? This was purely his doing." But somehow I knew where Sakeem was heading. Sakeem was saying I felt guilty somehow for what had happened.

Unintentionally, my voice had risen an octave as I exclaimed, "None of this makes sense!" Sakeem interjected, "It doesn't have to. You have taken on the belief that you, as all family members have, mind you, played a part; and if you had been a good, loving sister this would not have happened."

"Oh, God," A thick ugly layer of dread took hold. Intuitively, I knew what he said had been true. I whispered, "I had no idea that I was carrying these feelings. But you are correct: if I had been a better sister— a sister who loved her brother—perhaps talked to him or done something differently, maybe just maybe, he would still be here with us." I knew that Sakeem was right-on with this. Yet, never once had I formulated a conscious thought that revealed my true feelings.

"Would you allow me to say one more thing before we close for today, Nakala?" I waited for a minute before I answered him because honestly my heart hurt and the tears blurred my vision. My mind reeled with questions, but the one that surfaced first was, *Have I have been carrying feelings of guilt all of this time?* It seemed impossible to have had these feelings and never know it.

Sakeem waited for me for a few moments before he continued "Yes, well, when a family member passes—I refer to many causes of passing here—there are often feelings carried by the surviving family members like anger, guilt, shame, abandonment and so on which all result from fear. This is a program that was installed in mind long ago and carried over to this lifetime. These subtle memories or thoughts result in deeply embedded feelings that are often over looked. Nevertheless, they are there. Now you can openly ask yourself, 'If only I had done something different, perhaps things would have turned out better.'

"Nakala, I know you never really *liked* your brother. In your world he was wild and harsh. In addition, there are feelings of great anger and resentment that you carry for David's choice to check out of this life. You felt that, once again, he neglected his responsibilities just like he had while you were growing up; even though deep down you expected this behavior from him, you resented it!

"Your society has created a belief system that people are role models. Each of you plays particular roles according to your sexuality, age, education, family hierarchy and status, in say, the community and work place."

"In the family setting, an older brother's role is a protector, a confidant, someone who shares in particular tasks and responsibilities, just to name a few. In your mind, David didn't play his part correctly. As a result, you felt angry, cheated, abandoned and resentful toward him. More importantly, you felt betrayed by him—that you didn't have what society deemed proper and your inherited right—what you should have had was a healthy and happy family unit. Nakala, these are all beliefs and feelings that must be dealt with in order to heal in entirety."

I shook my head in disbelief at what Sakeem was telling me. I knew I was angry at David, but I had never connected the dots about being cheated that I didn't have a brother who cared enough to watch over me.

However, I knew that what Sakeem was stating was the absolute truth. David just wasn't there for me—except this one time and because of that one time, I think it made it worse. I had received an inkling of what it felt like to have a brother who cared—really cared.

It was when my oldest son passed. We were living in Olathe, Kansas. David and his young family were living in our small hometown, three hours away. His family made the trip for the funeral (the only time they ever visited us). We all had arrived at the church at the same time. Just as I stepped out of the car to go into the church, David met me and took me into his arms and held me tight. He was telling me that he loved me—that he cared. It was the only time that I felt like he truly loved me. Five years later David passed himself.

CHAPTER
SIX

Saturday night came and Nathanal reminded me that tomorrow was my day to spend with my Pleiadian parents, Sarah and Quem.

My Father, Quem had left Master Babaró in charge of me some time ago when they had been scheduled to return to Myra, Pleiades to see to their responsibilities.

Shortly before I took possession of my new home in California, Father Quem had announced that he and Mother Sarah would be coming to stay with me for a time. At first, when one of my guides would use this phrase 'for a time' I was baffled—as the phrase was ambiguous. But after hearing it countless times I came to accept that 'for a time' was like anything else. We can plan to do something for a certain length of time but really all is subject to change in a moment's notice.

Sunday morning came and I had an hour before my parents were set to arrive. I went about lighting my candles and incense and put on a CD to raise the vibration of not only the house but also me. I wondered if we would drive up Mt. Shasta this morning. (We had talked about it earlier.)

At 8:45 a.m. I heard Nathanal say, "They are here." Quickly, I finished up a few things, got my journal and a pencil then sat down to receive.

Father Quem chose to speak first, "Good morning, dearest Nakala. The day is beautiful! We choose not to go up on Mt. Shasta this day as it is shrouded—covered in a blanket of smoke, the result of the fires north of here. The wind sweeps the smoke to and fro until the energy has been transmuted. We desire you not to be in this as it is not healthy for you to breathe—driving would be a bit of a hazard as well. Therefore we keep you home to pray, study, relax and take care of you!

"This week has been evolutionary in terms of healing past hurts concerning family members. What you have learned regarding your brother applies to all members of your family, friends, as well as all peoples. You have judged each and every person who, in some measure, have not lived up to your expectations in some manner.

"Many times, we have worked on this subject, Nakala. I remind you that you, on this Earth plane are all recovering from past incidents and traumas. *All* are working toward healing and *all* are doing the best they can at the present moment. This is your level of awareness until your awareness expands. People cope with feelings of disappointment, anger and so on the way the best way they know how until they are ready to move forward and learn a better way.

"I go on…I speak on your biological Mother who is now 86 years of age. You have yearned for a closer relationship with her your entire life. Just this past year you laid down that desire, accepting that she is who she is. She feels more comfortable with her needle work than with people. Her art will not lash out and hurt her, my dear. Her art will not betray her in any manner or leave her…or so she thought. She feels safe with the yarn, the paints and so on.

"However, four months ago her home was devoured by the flames of a ravishing fire. Most of all her belongings were regarded as destroyed by smoke damage. This was devastating to her. Being from the era of the Depression she refused to accept this declaration from those in authority and made many attempts to retrieve her things. She felt she must save what gave her the most pleasure in life and disregarded her health by entering a house that was layered in black smoke. She cared so deeply for her things that she chose to ignore the warnings given to her by virtually everyone!

"You felt she disregarded everyone who loved her and wanted her to be safe and healthy—not breathe that awful pungent smell. For you, you saw that she cared more for things instead of for herself. For you this is quite amazing to witness. Time and again, you have plainly witnessed what you perceive as a crude devotion toward family and art—what she views as priority.

"I speak not of this to judge but to educate you. It has been the habit of the masses to judge others when they expect something of another and they do not receive it. You think you are one who does not hold grudge? Think again, Dear One. When you expect movement from another and they do not reciprocate for some reason (mind you, to you, it may be a justifiable reason), you have invisible blackboard where you make mark. Some of these marks are made in a very subtle manner but they are there. I see them—I feel them.

"If we, the Beings of Light were to make a mark when you do not think, feel or act accordingly to be in alignment with God, well, we would have stopped our work here to assist the peoples of the Earth long ago. In fact our work here would never have begun. Truth!

"I ask you, dear Nakala, not to give up on those you love. Please.

"I would not give you these words—this message—if you were not ready to receive in fullness.

"We move on just now. You are chosen scribe for the group Comterous that specializes in multi-media or the communications field. You have been sponsored by being chosen to channel messages and communications for not only yourself but for others, as well. You were told in the very first days, through your union with us, you would write many books. These books are for purpose many. The most important reason is to give forth the knowing that the people of the Earth have those, many, from the higher realms who are eager to give of themselves *freely*. The books are meant to give hope that the peoples on the Earth plane are going forward— are healing and evolving to a higher consciousness and vibration—are moving into the fifth dimension. Many of you are already vibrating at a fifth dimensional level. Truth!

"We have moved you here, to California to be surrounded by the mountains and to live on the mountain called Shasta. You have found yourself living at the base of this grand energy.

"The mountain of Shasta is a vortex. A vortex amplifies the energies of thought and emotions that is created by individuals and as a collective. (Remember the Nature Kingdom also thinks and feels as well.)

The energy here assists us greatly in amplifying our radiation, our intention. I also speak of the energies of astrological alignments, which are amplified greatly as well in areas such as these.

"On an educational note: what happens in this type of environment goes way beyond my previous statement.

"Last November you were given a precise directive—to leave Kansas City for the entire month of February 2014. You were to travel to Northern California, specifically to Mt. Shasta. You were told that you were to get out of Kansas City—the energy in this city would be shifting and you were not to subject yourself to it. The directive was a viable reason and you took it seriously.

"You took it upon yourself to openly disclose this information with members of your community. Because of this disclosure, three other persons decided to travel to Mt. Shasta as well. One joined you for the entire month (traveling with you across the country by vehicle), while the other two traveled by plane, staying for several days.

"You and your friends all have a long standing relationship with the Mt. Shasta area. I speak of the Lemurians who reside therein.

CHAPTER
SEVEN

"You are a Pleiadian traveler who came to this sweet Earth eons ago to assist those who had fallen into the dense energies—under a thick blanket of impenetrable fog, so to speak, where God had forsaken them, forgetting their existence, or so it seemed.

"You, Nakala, alongside of many others, chose to come here to assist by donning on the cloak of flesh—the human body. This was done because you have free will. It was your choice to do this. Consequentially, you made a commitment long ago that you would continue forth in this manner—the cycles of incarnating in the flesh—to assist those who had been caught in the web of lies that have been presented to them in a multitude of ways that stem from the belief that they are separate from God. Thus, you too were caught in the web of dark energy. You have been waiting for the opportune time to raise yourself up from the dense energies into the light with the assistance of those like ourselves who are dedicated, qualified and willing to do so.

"Our nation, the Pleiades, is strong beyond your present scope of reasoning. We are advanced beyond your understanding: technologically, mentally, and spiritually. Our comprehension of genetic structure/codes, which supersedes expertise on Earth in the scientific/medical fields, to this date exceeds your understanding and your research by well over two thousand years. We are at the forefront to show you the way. Ah, yes, there are others from faraway stars and planets who are here to assist as well.

"I speak of this because the Earth's people are in the process of waking up from their deep sleep/belief in God as a separate entity. The process is to reveal and to educate the peoples as they are ready to receive.

"As channel, Nakala, you are fully aware that there are many Higher Beings of Light who have dedicated themselves to this task—to assist until you no longer require this assistance and stand strong, united as One. "This brings me back to the Lemurians who live in the mountain called Shasta."

* * *

"The continent of Lemuria existed long ago off the western seaboard of what is now the United States. Lemuria was destroyed by a cataclysmic event. However, before this event took place, the high priests were warned that this event was imminent and to prepare themselves accordingly. So those of higher authority—the heads and bodies of many councils of which consisted of high priests, lords, masters, the king and queen, those of noble esteem—took it upon themselves to warn the people and protect their sacred teachings. They set about moving the sacred teachings, tools and flames to safer places in preparation for the upcoming devastating event. Many of the people themselves moved underground for protection not only for their physicality but for the sacred teachings.

"Unfortunately, not all were saved. You, as one of the priestesses, chose to comfort those as they departed from their earthy bodies. Consequently, you passed from that life as well. You were of a higher order, Miss and gave up your way of life, your memory, and your freedom that day in order to comfort those in great peril and distress.

"The Lemurians live underground for purpose to evolve. Meaning they choose to live apart from the surface people which include you, Nakala, in order to remain at a higher vibration. If they had chosen to live amongst you on the surface, they would have not been able to continue their steps as they have. In essence, they would have incurred a huge setback.

"Nakala, you, dwelt with these people, the Lemurians, for thousands of years. The Lemurians have always known that the day would come when they would emerge and join the surface people as all are United—All are One.

"Over the years, the Lemurian High Priest, Adama of the city of Telos, has shared communications with certain messengers revealing bits and pieces of information regarding their existence in preparation for the merge.

"Nakala, on your lower level of consciousness, you were made aware of their existence and their way of life just recently through the written word. On a higher level, you have always been aware and even have been in communications with them concerning the preparations that we speak of.

"When you read the texts channeled by Adama that were given to the masses, you felt in your heart that you were connected to these people, did you not?" My heart warmed as the memories reemerged and I replied, "Oh, yes, I did and the longing in my heart to return to these people has not lessened but only grown stronger."

Father Quem continued his story, "I speak on this community/city that the Lemurians created long ago because they are part of the hierarchy who are working to assist you with your trip to the fifth dimensional level of consciousness.

"You were chosen to come here to the Mt. Shasta area to assist in the educational dispensation that was gifted to the Masters. You are to assist by channeling messages given to you by not only us, the Pleiadians, those who travel the galactic highways, but also those who reside in the inner-earth, the Lemurians, as well."

Suddenly, my attention was drawn out the window and up in the sky. I saw several swirling dark gray-brown clouds of smoke that were rising quickly above the giant cedar and pine trees in my community. Oh, God! There is a fire. I got up and looked out my front door to see if I could get a better view. The smoke was billowing upwards and to the northeast. It looked like it is coming from town—my town.

Just moments ago, I was admiring how beautiful the clouds were and the breeze that had quickened, causing the pine needles to rain down on the red and white patio umbrella where I had sat earlier. Now, the wind posed a threat. All summer forest fires had been burning. I knew all too well the imminent danger. Immediately, I went into survival mode, fear— momentarily forgetting my lesson on the opportunities to renew.

PART
THREE

TRANSMUTING ENERGY

CHAPTER
EIGHT

Without prior notice, Mother Sarah took over the dictation. She said, "Nakala, dearest, I have stood beside your father, Quem for many years. He is my husband and I support him in all that he does. Make it known, that I have my own thoughts, my own opinions, as well, just as you do.

"It is time that I take a more active role with your training and the writing of the books that are being channeled through you."

Before she could continue her message, though, I was directed to get up and begin to gather my things should I need to leave my home.

Quickly, I grabbed my suitcase and began to throw things in it. I knew that there wasn't any logical sense to what I was packing because I didn't know *what* to pack. Then I began to ask Nathanal questions about what was most important to take with me. I felt rushed, out of sorts, and uncertain that I would be returning to this place. I felt like I was missing things that I would want later. Just a moment later, I heard Nathanal calmly take over to instruct me, "Only take what you need to survive—no more."

My focus changed to what I needed if the weather should turn colder, so I grabbed a heavy sweater and a raincoat. My pretty sweaters and jackets remained on the hangers. Then my neighbor, Karen, rang my door bell to let me know that we should be ready in case of an evacuation. She had wanted to linger and talk. I politely said, "Excuse me but I am going to continue to pack."

As soon as I had my car packed, I headed out only to find the highway was closed. By an unaware policeman I had been directed to a dead end. I had to get turned around. While I waited in traffic to turn around, a man about my age hollered across the street to ask where I was going. I hollered back, "I want to go south."

"Get on Old Stage Road."

"I don't know how to get there."

He was pointing northwest behind me, as he yelled, "Follow me. I'll get you on the correct road. I'll show you the way."

I knew Old Stage Road was in the other direction. A little voice inside of me was asking, "Should I trust this man or not?" It seemed to me that I didn't have any other options, so I got behind him and kept him in my sight the best I could.

In a matter of minutes, the man pulled off the road and pointed to a side road and then pointed to me. I waved and yelled, "Thank you!"

Finally, I was on Old Stage Road going south—the way I wanted to go. It wouldn't be long when I would find a ramp to get me on the highway—away from my new home—away from the fire. I knew there was a big possibility that I may never be back to live at my home again. I sighed pondering my new situation. *What is the real reason I have been brought to this place?*

* * *

The Farmer's Market is held on Mondays, in Mt. Shasta City a few miles south of Weed—the city that now was burning out of control.

Originally, I had planned to drive to Mt. Shasta and purchase my produce today. Now what? I wasn't sure what to do. I thought on it and decided to drive on in to Mt. Shasta. Maybe I'd talk to some locals who might know the situation. I took the Mt. Shasta exit and drove into town. As I looked for a parking place, I noticed the cloud formation on top of Mt. Shasta. The Cloud looked like a giant angel wing. It was beyond stunning. The sight prompted me to ask Nathanal, "Is the wing a sign? Are *they* (the Higher Beings of Light) here to help us?" In Nathanal's tone I heard respect and reverence like I had never heard before as he answered, "Oh, yes, you know not what is occurring. They are here watching over you—this place. Mt. Shasta is a sacred place. No harm shall come to the mountain."

After I did my shopping at the Farmer's Market, I took some pictures of the angel wing cloud and then went over to the local diner to eat. I reasoned that I had nowhere else to go. I was seated adjacent to a booth where five people sat, four men and a woman. The woman was on her cell phone, clearly upset, trying to talk the person on the other end into leaving—going somewhere safe. I knew she was talking about the fire in Weed. I sat there for a few minutes listening to the one-sided conversation when I found myself standing up and walking to their table, then asking about their situation. These people were in shock, having minutes ago seen their homes go up in flames; they didn't know what to do next. Neither did I. I gave them my condolences and decided it was time that I go find a place to stay for the night.

Heading south on highway 5 to Redding was the only thing I could think of to do. Redding was an hour away and the largest city that I knew that would have motels. However, fifteen minutes into my journey I heard, "Stop in Dunsmir. It would be good if you got a room there." I did as I was instructed but as soon as I heard the room rate, I politely said, "No, thank you."

For the next forty-five minutes I drove south to Redding, the next large city on corridor 5. I wanted cheap, so Nathanal took me straight to the Motel 6. I sighed. The sun had set. I didn't know my way around and I wasn't in the mood to try to find anything nicer.

After I got into my room, I remembered that Mother Sarah had been giving me a message just before I was directed to leave my home. I was tired and just wanted to take a steaming hot shower, go to sleep, and forget everything.

✳ ✳ ✳

Checkout time was 12:00 noon. I had no where I had to go and I was pretty sure from the sound of what was being reported on the Internet thread I wasn't going to return home anytime soon. The fire continued to rage and so far it didn't sound like they were letting people back into town.

However, shortly after I woke up I heard Nathanal directing me, "Get ready, we are leaving." Flabbergasted, I asked, "Nathanal, What?"

Nathanal didn't seem to take notice of my energy. "You heard me, we are leaving. We have things to do." I shook my head in utter disbelief. I had been looking forward to working on this crocheted shawl that I had started last week or maybe writing until noon but I didn't voice any of that. Instead, I muttered, "Okay." I reminded myself that there are often times like these that I just don't understand why I am directed to do certain things.

As soon as my car was loaded Nathanal directed me to go to the motel office and ask them about any reports on the fire. I wondered why but kept my questions to myself. (I knew Nathanal knew all about the fire.)

There wasn't anything new concerning the fire except that *maybe* some of the evacuations were lifted. All seemed to be conjecture. No matter what the reports said, the directive I was getting from Nathanal, my guide, was we were heading home. During the drive back home we did some sightseeing, made a few stops, all the while I was praying that I had a home to return to.

CHAPTER
NINE

When I drove down the last stretch of my road leading to my house, I marveled that the pines, cedars and the cypress trees still stood untouched by the fire. I smiled as I watched the black cows graze in the pasture and thanked God that the wild blackberry bushes still hugged the fence alongside the road just like everything was the same.

When I saw the open gate leading into my community, I said a silent thank you for keeping this place safe. The feelings of fear that my home would vanish had run deep. But as I saw that my home was safe, I remembered that love had persevered and always triumphs over all.

When I brought in my bags from the car, Nathanal said, "Leave them near the back door. You will feel better if things are ready in case you are told to evacuate again." In the background, I could hear the drone of the helicopters as they flew from the lake to fill up their buckets and take them to the areas that continued to burn.

Nathanal commented, "The fire still burns," then said, "Mother Sarah is ready for you when you settle yourself."

In a soft reassuring voice, I heard my mother say, "Nakala, my daughter only, it is time that I assist you with the writings. Please ready yourself to receive."

"To make it clear, I wish to explain the functionality of your father, Quem and myself. We work in many areas but our main objective as King and Queen of Myra, Pleiades is to maintain balance—remain sovereign—working in the galaxy to maintain the proper periphery."

"With these responsibilities comes the certainty that we have upcoming rule to take charge of our display of action. Meaning, we must have ones who are qualified, able and willing to take our place in the case any event occurs unforeseen or seen.

"You and Nathanal are our upcoming rule. You are willing, yes? Although at the present time, you see yourself as not qualified or able to fulfill this role. In response to being unprepared for future assignment, you are focused on completing tasks to fulfill your sacred contract and you have begun regimented—intensive—training five years past on this level of consciousness. This is to assist us in the movement to extend knowledge that there are a great many beings of light who work beside the peoples of the Earth—knowingly for some and unknowingly for others.

"On a conscious level, you, Nakala, know not *all* that is involved in our work. We are here to teach you. My role as mother and teacher, up to this point, has remained in the background. The time has come that I become an active participant in your training. It is so. I am taking the role as master writer for a time to assist you with the books. The others shall step aside while I am dictating."

Mother Sarah continued her transmission, "Look at what you have incurred in the last few days. I speak of the fires. What better way to train someone than through an actual experience? What better way to assist the people than to go out into the field and lend your hand?"

I had to give it to her, getting out in the field was the best way I knew how to train someone. I sighed, as I wondered what on earth I could do to help these people. I was sure, though, that all would reveal itself in the next few days.

✳ ✳ ✳

This morning, I awoke to an odd pinging noise. As I readied myself for the day, I thought I should go investigate what the noise was. As I walked out of the bathroom into the office to peer out the sliding glass door,

I saw that God had answered two of my prayers. The wind had died down and there was a gentle, steady rain gracing our land. God, I prayed that the rain would continue and even come down with a little more force.

I could still hear the helicopters in the distance traveling back and forth from the water source to the mountain where the fire continued to burn. What a monotonous task I thought…but then instantly, I realized the level of skill it would take for pilots to fly in adversity and under such pressure. Lives were always threatened when there is a wild fire. These people had to hit their target accurately, as every moment counted.

I heard my name being called, gently nudging me. "Nakala, it is time we get back to our reason for writing." "Yes," I said, "I suppose it is time." My heart expanded as I felt my mother's love pour through me.

"Nakala, I have given you reason for being in this area. There are hundreds of misplaced people with no plan as to where they are to go. Their homes are either damaged or gone completely. In addition, there are dozens of pets that need temporary shelter. Put your name on the list as one who is willing to serve. You are to go out and assist those in need.

"It is time we move on. However, I have one more thing to say before we do. Nakala, you asked that your home be saved. It was. You were given grace, my daughter. We are most grateful that you may continue your work from this locality in comfort and peace. You see, we have brought you here for many reasons. To work with the people who have lost their homes and their treasures is only a small portion of why you are here.

"I want to explain something to you," Mother Sarah continued. "The fires are for purpose, to transmute negative energy. For you, it seems this reason is implausible. Two days past, you witnessed firsthand the devastation the fire caused by destroying over a hundred homes and businesses—everything in its wake. Let's get down to it…cataclysmic events of any kind are destructive and reflect the very thoughts of the collective consciousness. The negative thoughts that are on-going must be dealt with—transmuted. Until you as a collective understand that this is a matter of cause and effect—that you are manifesting these events yourselves, these "natural disasters" will continue henceforth.

"When you were faced with the possibility that you may not have a safe place to rest when you returned to Weed, your blood ran cold with fear.

The fact is you ran well into the future, foreseeing something that had not yet happened."

Feeling the urge to defend myself I said, "I know that I fell into fear and I knew it at the time. However, the thing is that fire was so close to my house and the wind was whipping in all directions. It was all so unpredictable. Simply put, the odds were in the fire's favor. Because I am human, I have a mind and a brain. I knew all of this and I felt on some level I had to sort out my options…for any preserved scenario. I should have a plan well devised in case my home was damaged or destroyed. At the same time I knew I would be guided for the higher good in any case. I am still learning."

Mother Sarah remained silent for a few moments. I thought maybe she had gone, leaving me alone with my thoughts. I emptied my mind waiting for her to pick up where she left off, only to have the vision of my being on the road with my suitcases with my most important possessions for the last three and a half months take hold. During that time, I had no place to call my home and depended on friends and motels for security and comfort.

While on my travels, I had discussed my precarious position (living out of my car) with a few people. I had joked that I was free of responsibility, specifically free of the burden of utility bills, homeowner's insurance, maintenance and even property taxes. It felt good not to have those bills to pay—I was not responsible for any real property except for my car. I didn't mind that lifestyle all that much as long as the money held out. However, deep down a part of me wanted stability—a place I could return to that was safe and comfortable—a place that was mine.

Mother Sarah had remained quiet for me to review my thoughts and feelings. When I left my house during the worst part of the fire, I had gone into fear because I had left a few of my things behind—some clothes, all of my spiritual journals, (except for two) and all of my crystals. Although, I knew that leaving that stuff behind—not having it anymore—was not all that important…not really.

Then Mother Sarah spoke, "Nakala, leaving those possessions behind was not the entire reason you went into fear. You were fearful that you would not have a structure for stability to return to. If the structure were not there what would you do? Would you rebuild, find another place, or return to Kansas? When you asked yourself these questions you saw yourself as a failure who in essence would have to eat her words. You had worked to build up this place, California, making it sound attractive to yourself and to others all in order for you to feel good about your move here. In essence, it was a way to gain permission from not only your family and friends, but for permission by you to leave Kansas and all you were familiar with and start anew. Now what? Your own town caught fire. In addition, in Northern California there are other wildfires burning out of control. The residents are on constant alert. In addition, California is in the middle of a drought. Then there is the fact that Mt. Shasta is an active volcano. I ask you, what did you see here that was so perfect that you had to move here? Where is the stability in this place?"

Pausing for a while just to find the answers to Mother Sarah's questions, I realized that no place is a sure thing…not here or anywhere else. After I thought about what Mother Sarah had asked, I questioned where I had put my faith and replied, "Maybe I am putting all of my faith in a physical building instead of God. We are here to have experiences to learn from. We are here to remember we are not separate from God. God is in all of creation." I took a deep breath and sighed because I felt like I was not getting the whole picture here. I continued to plod through my thoughts and said, "Okay, we are manifesting our reality from our thoughts and feelings. I know that. So in conclusion, concerning this fire, we created it from our own fears."

I felt like I understood most of why the fire started but still felt like there may be more. Mother Sarah then said, "Nakala, you, as a collective are creating the fires from negative thought. Everyone must get on board and look at the positive in all of creation in order to manifest a positive outcome."

Suddenly, Mother Sarah shifted the subject. "I'd like to look at your feelings concerning why you wanted to move here." For some unexplained reason I felt timid and unsure of myself like I were in the hot seat but I went ahead and answered, "I came here because last February, when I was here visiting, I felt like this was home to me. I fell in love with this place. One day, as I gazed at Mt. Shasta, I specifically heard a voice say, 'It is time you came home.' Immediately, after that I began getting information on when I was to be here and what I needed to do to make it happen. On the flip side, I was incredibly torn to leave my family. I felt like I was doing something very wrong by moving so far away from them. But the feeling in my heart persisted. The feeling was incredible and I *had* to follow it."

I went on, "I love it here. The beauty here is incredible—peaceful. When I look at the mountains, trees, and sky, my love expands and literally I feel like I am in paradise. There is absolutely nothing like this in Kansas."

Mother Sarah said, "You were guided here for many reasons. One being you resonated with the energy here. There is a feeling of peace and that feeling is imperative in order to raise your consciousness and your vibration. You are ready for this step, Nakala. Yes, you felt torn by coming here. Anyone in your situation would have feelings of this nature. Part of you felt you were abandoning those dearest to you. Who wouldn't? But in order to be able to control the outer senses you must have peace. In order to draw from the inner self, you must have peace. To live in chaos inhibits and may even conclude the progression of raising your consciousness.

"We desire greatly that you live amongst people. However, you would do better, for now, with people who are like-minded. Make no mistake, family is most important but you were not objective with your biological family as you were too close and what you wanted for them yes, was stability, but you were in judgment of their lifestyle. Do you understand? Remember this is common, on some level, within all families.

"I make it simple. Unfortunately, every time you had a family discussion or gathering you were, in some way, drawn into the drama. The lot of you through thought, emotion, and action created drama and then *again*, through thought, emotion, and action proceeded to escalate it.

"Dear One for the highest good you were to leave so you could focus on your thoughts and emotions full-time. This is for you to integrate, in fullness, these teachings. I love you, my daughter, beyond measure. I, too, only want what is for your highest good. Because you have asked for our guidance, we are able to give it to you. Your family in Kansas has yet to ask. We continue to pray for their highest good that they open their hearts and minds to the spiritual teachings—the universal laws—God's Truth."

CHAPTER
TEN

"As you know the Boles Fire continues," began Mother Sarah's teaching. "The news is another fire south of here has started in the Sacramento area. This one has burned quickly and sounds much worse than what you are experiencing in the northern part of California. The way to get nature to respond in a positive manner is to love it. Send your love to the areas—to the nature spirits. All is consciousness. When you work in a positive manner you are transmuting negative energy yourself. I give you this task. I know this to be an easy one for you as your love expands greatly when you gaze at the trees, the rocks, the mountains, the sky—all of it!

"Being new to the area, you look upon the vista with a fresh perspective; with a higher appreciation. There is an elevated possibility that people who have been living in this area of California for an extended period are not marveling at what is before them simply because they have grown accustomed to their surroundings—the newness has worn off, you may say. Yes, they love their land but have grown familiar and are set in their particular habits—their daily tasks at hand. Nakala, you are like a young child who is seeing everything for the very first time. I see you become excited when you see even a new bud form on a plant. Do you see?"

Mother Sarah did not wait for my answer, but continued on with her teaching. "Use your new found appreciation to love the nature spirits.

Talk to them. Go out and hug a tree and tell the tree your feelings for nature. The tree will share your messages with all of nature as All are One."

"Go out tomorrow and begin to establish this communication with the trees and all of nature, making it part of your daily routine. Not only will nature get the message that you are here and you love them, but the tree will assist in grounding you and releasing old negative energy. Ask the tree to assist you in this way. As you release the old energy the tree will take it and send it into the earth to be transmuted. Remember to fill up the space you have created with love. Nakala, you will find that your day will flow easily when you partake.

"Ah, I hear your father, Quem, calling me. Perhaps it is time to lay down the pen and paper for now. I will check in with you tomorrow morning."

* * *

As suggested one of the first things I did that morning was step outdoors to hug one of the older larger cedar trees that grew near my home. As I got closer, I was drawn in by the irregular pattern of the rough bark. I touched the bark with my fingers before I leaned into the trunk with my frame surrendering to its energy. As my body touched the trunk I felt a distinct merge of the two of us. My heart connected with the tree; and even without asking, I felt a noticeable amount of the heaviness being lifted from me. In that moment, I knew that everything was right with the world and with me.

When I came back into the house, the first thing I heard was Mother Sarah say in her special way, "Thank you for following my directive, Nakala. Know that my instructions are always meant to assist you on your way to a higher perspective—an expanded level of awareness. This in turn, opens up the avenue to a superior current of the Divine Cosmic Energy that flows through you. You feel it now. In essence, your vibration has quickened and you are in a state of pure peace and love. I am pleased."

Mother Sarah ended her dialogue, and I sat there at my kitchen table it seemed for several minutes waiting for her to continue her message. However, she didn't.

I was completely content just sitting at the table gazing out the window although, I felt a bit torn, anxious in a way, feeling that I should be writing as I waited for Mother Sarah's next words. My inner voice whispered that perhaps that is what I should do—just sit here and enjoy the scene that was taking place outside of my window.

Mother channeled a deep breath through me signaling me to relax and said, "God is everywhere…in everything." As if Mother Sarah didn't want to disturb the forces of nature her voice softened almost to a whisper, "The birds have returned, Nakala. The rain showers received yesterday morning indicate new life and abundance for all. The prayers were heard, Miss, by the rain spirits and they happily responded."

Mother Sarah's next words perplexed me. "The flame of your candle burns nigh. What is your desire in this moment?" I didn't really know what to say because I was torn between my perceived task at hand—the writing—and the beauty of the great outdoors that easily entertained me.

I really wanted to sit and do absolutely nothing. But Mother Sarah was here to dictate information for the book. I felt like I didn't dare tell her that I wanted to relax. Even though I knew she is completely connected to what I am thinking and feeling, I avoided being my authentic self by answering, "Oh, just sitting here gazing out my kitchen window I feel at peace."

In reality, as if captivated with a good novel nearing the climax, I had been watching a large gray squirrel's ineffective attempt to scare the black birds away from where *he* considered *his* storage area to be. For several minutes this had been going on, and the squirrel just couldn't seem to get his point across. It was comical to watch the birds casually hop a few feet away from the squirrel to go about their business of foraging instead of taking flight. I was totally amused with the scene before me. Yet I lied, "You know, I really do not have any desires at this moment, Mother, other than to sit here and write with you."

Her response was "I am well aware that you are enthralled with the wild life there. Writing is at this moment a tedious chore that you think you are to complete and not what is truly your heart's desire. I gave you ample time to assess your thoughts and feelings. You knew before you spoke that your true desire was to be amused by the scene as it unfolded. I'd like you to remember this feeling—that all is well in the world and there is nothing in this moment more important than to feel the love." "Mother,"

I began, "I can see that if I felt like this all the time, I would not get much accomplished. However, to sit and be in this moment is what genuinely gives pleasure to me the most."

"Yes, my daughter. Nevertheless, we do have work to do. The writings are important as they are for purpose to help ease the pain and suffering in the world. Let us begin in earnest. You are near community that has suffered much this past week. You are part of this community even though you have only been here three weeks. You have only met people casually through your various errands around town and through meeting a few of your neighbors. You haven't been here long enough to make personal friends of a lasting kind. All of that will change before long." The way my mother was talking made me wonder what she was getting to. *Is my mother trying to comfort me or perhaps encourage me? Maybe she is just making conversation.*

"No, my Nakala, I am not merely making conversation for the sake of having something to say. This is nothing of the sort. What I am doing is showing you what step you are at in this exact moment concerning making relationships in this community. Because you do not have *real* companions of any sort in the physical realm, you do not feel a part of this place. What I mean to say is you have not found your purpose concerning the community."

I was beginning to see her lesson unfold as she continued her dictation. "Mother, I have met a couple of my neighbors and already feel like I could call them for any reason or just visit them. The owners of the park, where I live, watch over us like a mother and father would. I am making friends; I am not concerned at all with my progress."

"Nakala, there is a wide assortment of communities. You have this one where you live. There are spiritual communities where you can get together with like-minded people for different discussions and events. There are communities for artists, gardening, hiking, dancing, and politics. The list goes on. There are opportunities grand to join with various communities in creating something that is dear to your heart—that you treasure. I ask you again, what is it you desire?" I saw what Mother Sarah was driving at. She was asking me to decide what I wanted to be involved with that would make me happy.

"Yes," she said as she nodded her head. "I want you to get yourself involved with a community that is working together for a common good—to create something that stimulates and satisfies."

With that Mother Sarah announced that she was finished for today. Being surprised at how short our session was I began to argue, "Wait, we only just got started an hour ago. You are kidding, right?"

I saw her shake her head, no, before she responded, "I will be off for a few days. Your moving truck arrives early Monday from Kansas. I expect you will be busy with that. Remember that feeling of love that we were talking about earlier. That is all for now. I love you, dearest. I will be checking in periodically. Don't hesitate to call on me or your father."

No more words were spoken between the two of us. I simply got up and went outdoors to work for several hours raking up brown pine needles, twigs and bits of pine cones that the previous few days of high winds had knocked loose.

I felt like I lived in a magical kingdom. Through the stand of tall conifers, sycamores and oak trees I had a wonderful view of the mountains of Shasta and his counterpart Shastina. The grandeur of it all simply stupefied my senses.

CHAPTER
ELEVEN

For the past week no one had summoned me to get my computer out to work on this book. Last Monday, as expected, my furniture had arrived. With that delivery, I had a higher appreciation for the conveniences of home that before I had taken for granted. Each box that I had unpacked was like a long anticipated treasure adding color, texture and comfort to my days. Finally, after over three months, I had my things again. I especially was grateful for my bed. How sweet it was to have a little bonus in one's life.

Even though no words were received from Mother Sarah during this time I knew that she was near. There were moments throughout the day when I could sense her energy—her love.

During my time off, Babaró told me that Mother Sarah would be joining me to write Monday morning, specifically 11:00 a.m. Sometimes, I felt it was strange to meet with the Pleiadians like this, to work with them.

For three days, now, the skies had been overcast and rainy. Two days ago, I looked out the window to see Mt. Shasta and saw the peak was covered in a fresh layer of snow. What a glorious site after being barren for so many months.

*　*　*

"I am here. I am ready to begin anew," my mother announced. My heart expanded as I wondered what topic she would choose to talk on.

Mother Sarah said, "There is cause for celebration. Is there not? One of your friends from Kansas has found his way to Mt. Shasta City. He is on his way to fulfilling his sacred contract. There are two more who are working toward making this journey. Soon the four will be complete."

"When the four of you came out last February, each and every one of you heard the call to come. What you heard specifically was, 'Nakala, It is time to come home.' "Later you were directed to be here up and operational by October 1. Today is September 29. You have one day before you officially report for duty."

"You are to work with the community of Telos of which resides inside of the mountain called Shasta—in the inner Earth." Mother Sarah paused to let me examine her words. I knew that I would be working with them somehow as I had already been receiving communications from some of the residents as far back as 2010. Sakeem, Jonson, Tabitha and Jeremie are some of the beings who reside in Telos who had been in constant contact with me. Sakeem who is also a resident of Telos, moved in with me almost a year ago and had been working with me ever since.

In Mother Sarah's last statement, the word community nearly jumped off the page. She had been teaching on that subject the last time we had written together. After some reflection I had pinpointed that one of the communities I want to be involved with was Telos.

The idea that people live inside of a mountain (a volcano at that) seems beyond far-fetched even for this area. I had heard some of the locals speak about Telos. Some believed that the Lemurians and Telos is just a part of mythology. Others strongly believed that Telos is a fully functioning city that is as real as Mt. Shasta City, and one day soon we will merge with them.

I felt a strong pull from these beings. Perhaps *pull* isn't the correct term. Maybe I should say energy. Yes, I feel this incredible energy that I can't shake, like a magnetic force that clearly indicates that I am to learn from these beings. It is time to connect and unite.

I heard Mother Sarah say, "Nakala, it is time that we discuss the people who live deep in the mountain we call Shasta." "Mother," I began, "Before we get started I'd like to clarify something. When you talked about community the other day, was it your aim for me to identify my priorities when it comes to community? I want to be a part of several communities but the one that really calls me is Telos. I know they can teach me how to grow and prepare the produce I require in order to thrive and live in this physical body for hundreds if not thousands of years. They can teach me disciplines that would assist me in so many areas."

"Nakala," Mother Sarah said "It is time you know another piece of why you have been chosen to come to the mountain to live out your days." At this juncture, I could not imagine Mother saying anything concerning my move that I didn't already know.

"You have been given tidbits of information here and there concerning the whys of your stay here. You have come to cleanse yourself of all misaligned energy that resides in your bodies. Being in the mountains in nature is for you the highest good. The fresh air, for one thing, purifies. The soil and water here are clean. We have placed you here in a home without other people in human form. Yet your home is full of people who are from the higher realms—star beings who are fifth dimensional beings and higher. You have archangels about. You have come to meet some of the elementals who reside in the area. You are literally surrounded by those who love you and are teaching you for the highest benefit for not only you but for the collective. I ask you to understand that we can teach you exactly what the Lemurians can. It is not time for you to join with them as you are here on the surface of the Earth for a specific purpose. The purpose is to further culminate the realization and acceptance of the star beings who are here to assist the collective in their evolutionary process—the ascension.

"All peoples of this world are not only to know of us but also to be able to ask us for assistance, allow it to come forth, and to accept it with love. We must teach them that they are not here to live out a mundane existence but to fulfill their heart-felt dreams and live in peace not war. You are to live in prosperity not lack. You are to work with one another in harmony. You are to love one another in totality." "I understand this, Mother," I said, "but honestly the big thing here is how we get to this place of loving one another when we are constantly bombarded on every front with chaotic energy."

I stopped to assess my thoughts before continuing, "I feel like one of the reasons I came to California was to get way from the negativity so I can stop reacting to it."

I expected my Mother to pick up the conversation here but she didn't. *Why not?* The longer I sat reading my last sentence the more I wondered what I was missing. Then it hit me full force. I am creating the negative energy myself. *How do I stop the cycle?*

I was able to recognize easily when people go into drama or what I sometimes referred to as *their story* and was able to just move on without saying anything; but I still knew I was reacting with my thoughts and feelings. Sometimes, even with my own family if they didn't do something I thought they should, like say, 'thank you' I reacted and went into judgment. I had been doing it without realizing it. I couldn't get away from the negativity, not even here, as long as I was creating it myself! I had to change the way I think. It was all so convoluted! I felt the love of my Mother raise my vibration and knew that I would get this somehow.

Mother Sarah knowingly nodded her head, yes. I was wondering how these beings had so much patience for me as I sorted through my thoughts and feelings when I heard, "We love you without condition. You are on a particular level of awareness. We see you blossom before our very eyes. We know that your greatest *desire* is to become the embodiment of love in its fullness. Why else would you want to go to Telos and learn from the Lemurians? Why else would you have moved so very far away from your own flesh and blood?

"Nakala, at this moment I'd like to say that to come here was a great gift to yourself. You obeyed your Higher Self in coming here to learn to align and balance the bodies that comprise the totality of you. With this task you are assisting in balancing this world. In addition, you have made a huge sacrifice in coming here as you have moved from your biological parents, children, and grandchildren. You know that all people in your family did not wish to see you move away. I speak on these things because there is hurt associated with this move and a sacrifice. It could not be avoided.

"During the time when Jesus walked the Earth, he traveled to far off and exotic places. He was in training! He left his family—his parents, wife and children on numerous occasions. It was part of his sacred contract. We are discussing the ascension.

"Yes! All masters must train. All masters must know when it is time for this to occur. Honestly, when you have reached this place in your life when you accept that there is more to you than a physical body, when you find you are a divine matrix that comprises many bodies, when you learn it is time to align with your Higher Self and work for the highest good, the moments of fear which result in chaotic energy are created less and less. You are able to focus on the beauty in life and not the illusion of separation from God or any other intelligence or life form. We are All One and we are eternal beings. You are always connected. Always.

"I desire to get on with why you are here. Adama, the High Priest of Telos knows of you. He knows of your arrival. He is the one who sent Sakeem, Jonson, Tabitha and even Jeremie to stand beside you and work with you when the alignment to do so is complete. Sakeem has continually assessed your energy level and assisted you in numerous areas to lift you up in order for you to remain in the human form. I do not speak of this lightly. He assists you by giving you radiation to help ease your days and activate certain areas of the mind and DNA in order for you to go forward on your sacred journey. Sending Sakeem to your side was a definite addition to our team, Telbar. We thank Adama for his vigilance and honor him.

"You have grown quite fond of Sakeem. Yes?" I shook my head yes and waited for my emotions to calm down before I could answer. "Oh, yes, I have grown accustomed to having Sakeem around. I am grateful for his dedication and his never-ending love. I am aware that he assists Adama. However, I don't know what exactly he does for Adama."

I stopped and thought about how involved the people of Telos were with me before I spoke. "The others, Jonson, Tabitha, and Jeremie keep in contact with me but not like Sakeem. They come by and say hello. I do not know what area they work in either. Jonson, in particular, will come and say, *Hello Darlin'* I know it is he because in the beginning it was established that is how he would address me. He has this Texas drawl. I always say, hello. But then he usually doesn't say anything else. So I continue on with whatever I am doing. Maybe I am being rude. Maybe they are waiting for something, but I really don't put too much energy toward it. I mean if they want to talk to me they can."

"Nakala," Mother said, "These people are with you for several reasons: one being to help ease the transition of your move and another to assist with the transition of learning to work with light beings who travel the galactic highways." I stopped and thought about what she had said before I asked, "How are they helping me learn to work with others?"

"All beings have a particular personality which radiates energy. You are learning how to recognize these beings without seeing them with your physical eyes. You listen for the tone of voice—the energy behind the voice. Oft times, you will see an image in your inner eye that will give you a clue. Jonson is a cowboy and he dresses the part; he talks like he is from the south. This is the signature or personality he has chosen that sets him apart and assists you in recognizing him. With many, the personality is not disclosed and you are left thinking that the person may be stoic—that there is nothing distinct about them. They may have little or no sense of humor. I say this is quite possible, but more likely it is a matter of getting to know the person. So you see all that you are experiencing is showing you how things work in the higher realms. When Jonson, Tabitha and Jeremie are ready to work on a specific level that you are able to detect, you will know. Perhaps they are friends of yours from long ago here to reestablish connection."

✳ ✳ ✳

I thought we were finished with the session when I heard Mother Sarah say, "I'd like to change the topic of conversation."

"Of course."

Mother Sarah began by saying, with much feeling, "Today is a special day." Then paused for effect before continuing on, "I'd like you to reflect on those words and allow the energy behind those words to build." I felt my vibration rise as I thought about the words *special* and *day*, feeling the anticipation of what this day would most certainly bring. Mother Sarah had stated, with confidence and a knowing, that there *was* something going to happen today or maybe even several things that were special that were sure to come. A surge of happiness and joy arose leaving me full of wonder and expectation. To further assimilate what the statement conjured up, I began to sort out my thoughts and feelings out loud. "To me the word *special* evokes memories of surprises and gifts. Because of your simple yet palpable statement, I find myself looking forward to what this day most assuredly is bringing. I am feeling excited!"

"Yes, when you hear the statement, 'Today is a special day,' especially when it is said by someone of authority, you put more stock in it. In essence, in your mind, this person is allowing or creating an activity or event that is well out of the ordinary and to be treasured, like a celebration of some sort that you may be an integral part of. However, I want you to take note that it is the person who is in charge who is creating the special part of the day, not you.

"Let's switch it up a bit shall we? I'd like you to incorporate this affirmation in your morning ritual. You can say it like I have stated previously, 'Today is a special day,' or like this, 'I am creating a special day.' In this case, *you* are the one of immense and grand authority as you are the creator of your reality.

"I encourage you to pay close attention to the energy that these words arouse. Let your energy build—allow your imagination to take flight, as well, to the possibilities that may come, knowing with that energy (those thoughts and feelings) you are creating whatever you put your mind to—you are magnetizing this reality into your field, your life. This is the Law of Attraction.

"I must add that you are continuously drawing to you anything you think and feel. The purpose of this exercise is to focus on the positive. The more you do this the more conscious you become when you are creating positive or negative thoughts. Thus you are mastering the art of controlling your energy."

CHAPTER
TWELVE

The days had cooled somewhat and some of the vegetation was beginning to turn from the various shades of greens to the fall colors of reds, oranges and yellows. Like a young child who anticipates anything new, I was looking forward to the changes of the seasons.

As I was finishing up with the dishes, I saw out my window a hard-working grey squirrel digging yet another hole along the edge of my concrete driveway. Because every day I find additional freshly dug holes in the flower beds and even the lawn, I had wondered if they dug these holes just for the sake of digging. This time, however, I saw him get a nut out of the hole. I had to say, my yard is well aerated.

Quietly, I chuckled as I dried the last plate and put it away. As I hung up the dish towel, I felt a slight pressure on my shoulder and asked, "Nathanal is that you?" "Yes, Miss," was his answer.

I turned to face him, seeing only my kitchen cabinets—a room void of another living being. Without thinking, I let my inner knowing take over to see my Nathanal and was surprised that I saw him so easily. I smiled and said, "Oh, there you are, Nathanal."

I am unable to see him physically, but I was able to sense where he stood. "What is it Nathanal?" But instead of hearing an answer, I saw in my mind's eye his form. He was about a foot taller than I, slender, but had a muscular build. I smiled again as I saw his shoulder-length curly brown hair. I caught his over-sized clear blue eyes as he gazed into mine. Nathanal was grinning like he was up to something—no good. I laughed and continued to study his facial features. It wasn't often that I got such a good look at my counterpart—my twin flame. That smile… *Oh, Nathanal what are you up to?*

Nathanal's nose is slender and he sported a neatly trimmed mustache and beard. He wore a soft white linen pullover tunic with loose-fitting pants of the same fabric. On his feet were modest brown sandals that looked similar to flip-flops only there was this funny little brown tassel attached to them. There on his chest lay the unmistakable Akasie emerald (approximately an inch in diameter) and I gasped as the light danced off the facets. I marveled at its size and quality.

Those higher in the Akasie line wear the Akasie emerald. The emerald is a symbol of power and honor, and those who wear it are highly respected. I was silently reminded of who we are once again.

I had been looking back up into Nathanal's sparkling eyes when I saw and felt the magnitude of his love. He smiled. Oh, God I love this man-angel. Then I blurted out, "Why am I able to see you so clearly today? Are you projecting the image or…how is this working?" Nathanal did not speak just held out his hands for me to take, which physically I could not.

Without any prior indication of what was to happen, I saw myself reach out outside of my body and take his hands I felt the electricity pulsating as he pulled me closer into his embrace. My heart raced as I watched myself merge with his energy. I didn't understand what was happening but I saw and felt it in a primal way. A single guttural moan escaped my lips that sounded like it had come from a faraway time and place. The sound had revealed something indecent, wanton, and almost pitiful in me. Because of that I felt embarrassed that he had heard me lose control of my faculties. Yet I stayed with the embrace for a few moments longer.

I wasn't comfortable with what was occurring, so I pulled away and asked, "Nathanal, what is happening? I don't understand this." A deep breath was channeled through me telling me to relax. I couldn't hold the tears back any longer and I heard myself begin to sob. Suddenly, with a fury I didn't know I held, I cried out to God in a voice that held back nothing, "Why, God, does it have to be this way?" I shook my head and turned away from Nathanal as I tried to hide my vulnerability—my over-powering feelings of hopelessness and desperation in the situation. With my entire being, I wanted-needed Nathanal by my side as a mate should be in a physical body. I felt the gentle pressure of Nathanal's hand on my shoulder once again and I shuddered.

Nathanal's voice was soft as a whisper, "Nakala, I love you. You are my wife, my counterpart. There is nothing I want more than to stand by your side and assist you in this journey."

No demands were made; no judgments voiced. What I was feeling I could not describe as it was a jumbled mess that screamed to be let loose. However, I could not. Quickly, I made my exit to go outdoors, rake the lawn, and lose myself in some physical release through hard work.

⁕ ⁕ ⁕

Two hours later, the vulnerability, shame and primitive want had been temporarily set aside—forgotten. The air had cooled and the sun had begun its descent. I put away my garden tools and headed into the house. While I had been working, I had sensed Nathanal sitting on the front porch calmly watching me—waiting for me to come back to him.

When I walked in the house, out-loud I announced that I was back and that I would be taking a shower—that I hoped to talk to *someone* about what had happened earlier when I returned. I didn't wait for an answer. I just kept walking.

After my shower, I felt refreshed and ready to return to the living area. I sat down on the couch, and I reached for my journal to work out my thoughts and questions on paper regarding this out of body experience. From what I had concluded, my etheric body works independently, separately from my physical body but was acting out my sub-conscious desires or maybe my conscious desires. But I couldn't be sure. Laying down my pencil, I waited for Babaró, Samuel Paul or Mother Sarah to speak to me.

It was Mother Sarah who chose to give me words that would ultimately calm my fears. "Nakala, darling, I would love to ease your uncertainty by answering your questions concerning what transpired previously." I quickly grabbed a tissue as the first tear rolled down my cheek. "Mother," I confided, "I love Nathanal but I feel so alone here. I don't have anyone in the physical to care for me—hold me. I know God does not intend that I go through my life without a man…yet I have Nathanal. Do you see what I mean?" I didn't pause long enough for her to respond but kept speaking. "And then that thing happened when I felt myself reach out of my body and *touch* Nathanal." An uncomfortable laugh escaped my lips as I realized that I was a bit embarrassed to talk to her, or anyone, for that matter, about my desires as a woman. I had specifically chosen the word *touch* to adequately diminish, to my satisfaction, what had occurred between Nathanal and I.

"Nakala, darling," Mother began again, "You are wife to Nathanal and the love beckons you. You have desires as does your Nathanal. Just because he is unseen to you in the physical realm does not mean he is unfeeling. Do you understand, Nakala?" With that, I said, "I don't think I want to talk about this." I was truly mortified that I was having this dilemma.

"Nakala," Mother said in a strong voice, "You are to understand what is happening and this is to be put down on paper for others to read. My aim is to assist you in sorting out this experience. I am your mother and this is one of my functions."

I wasn't responding to Mother Sarah's directive that I was to put *this* down on paper, so she continued her say. "Honey, I know this is difficult for you, but it is for the highest good for you to understand and integrate the transitions that are occurring at this time. You are awakening to your higher God-Self and abilities that have been long forgotten." I managed to mumble, "Okay," as I reached for another tissue.

"For now, I will not get into so much detail that you are weighed down. As I was explaining beforehand, you and Nathanal are husband and wife—twin flames—a very special team. You work with each other *always*. Your energies are merged together—married—bonded, if you will, in a lasting fashion.

"When I speak of marriage, some people may misunderstand and may think that the marriage I speak of is merely a piece of paper or a verbal agreement that basically may be easily disregarded or broken.

"I will give you this example. Take two pieces of metal that have been forged together, literally fusing it, making it one. No matter what tools you use or how much force you apply to separate the two pieces of metal, the bond will not ever be broken. The two pieces of metal cannot be separated. You may bend the metal but the bond holds true.

"After you were breathed from God as a spark of energy the single spark drew apart making two aspects: the male and female parts. (This did not happen until much later through the evolutionary process.) Together you make one. Together you complement each other in such a way that you make whole—complete.

"You hear many spiritual leaders speak the words, 'We are One?' You hear us use this phrase frequently, as well. This is the same principal. All are created by the divine spark of God—the same energy—all work together to go forward as one entity or the collective.

"We all work together in some fashion but you and Nathanal are two parts of the same flame and resonate at a much higher level. You are literally the same but have embodied different aspects, attributes, skills and experiences.

"We are always evolving whether it is in a human body or some other state of being.

"Currently, you and Nathanal are working together to assist each other in the teachings—the lessons that are given in this grand place called the Earth—to master the control of energy in the human form. (This is happening on a larger scale with all intelligences and life forms as well. However, the teachings with Nathanal are on a much more intimate level.)

"Now, you and Nathanal can take on any role, like a husband or wife, a mother or father and so on. You may present yourself as friend, neighbor, acquaintance or possibly a co-worker (there are a multitude of possibilities). Some incarnations you may or may not recognize one another fully. This go-around (incarnation) Nathanal is working from the unseen realms or the higher realms as you walk the Earth plane. You have been gifted with the knowledge of who he is precisely, as he presents self as your guide.

"To go further, Nathanal stays by your side most always. There are times when he is called to some other locality for a particular reason (as you call it, to check things out), before you travel. The truth of the matter is he is involved in many areas of teaching for you, always looking ahead to ensure that you take the correct steps to keep you on your sacred path.

As Nathanal assists, he is learning as well. You both are evolving and going forward.

"There are other masters who assist and direct in a multitude of areas in your evolutionary process. As a whole, our group, Telbar (those joined for the common cause to assist you with your ascension) works to avoid giving you too much information, thus becoming a tedious affair for you. It is best to allow you to work on your level and not be concerned about how we conduct ourselves by what lessons we are giving forth at any given moment.

"However, there are times (many as of late), when your mind has become stimulated; expanding in such a way that you want to know how things work. This is fine and to be expected. You are expanding your consciousness and with that you have come to realize that so many other ways of doing things are possible. You have found that in the past, as individuals, and also as a collective, you have somewhat limited your imaginations, thus, creating barriers from attaining a way of life that pervades God's truths with peace and harmony—a grand love that surpasses all.

"In other words, you have held belief systems that have kept you in check and limited. It is time that you freed yourself by reprogramming yourself. As you gain mastery over the divine matrix of your being, the confining weights of limit are being lifted and you are truly remembering that you are beings of the infinite—anything is possible.

"I wish, Dear One, that you not get too caught up in the mechanics of how we do our work. Just know if you have a desire, any desire, hold vigilant the knowing—the intent—that to receive is possible.

"Please focus on what is for your highest good and know that the teachings will continue. Your true reason for being is to have the experience of living in a human body and to control energy for the highest good through that body.

"You are the living breathing embodiment of God. God has chosen this particular expression—to live through you! You are a powerful being; yet you do not remember. I have an unsurpassed perspective as I watch you go through your life maneuvering throughout your daily challenges as you continue to hold vigilant your focus on your life's sacred journey. As your Pleiadian Mother, I am pleased to have this opportunity to share God's creation through His many and vast experiences."

THIRTEEN

I had gone to the kitchen to take a break from writing and was busy cutting up veggies for my lunch when two random questions popped into my mind. One: Why after five years had Mother Sarah suddenly decided it was time to work with me? Two: Why had mostly men been assisting me and teaching me instead of women?

Except for the very first few months after I had begun to hear my guides, the masters and the angels, I had always had men assisting me and teaching me except for a few instances. Tirclé had been one exception, coming to me on several occasions to channel drawings through me.

On occasion, a woman would make herself known and say something polite but never work with me on a level that I knew of. Then I heard Mother Sarah say, "That would be a good topic to discuss…after lunch."

As my lunch ended, I began to shift my thoughts to my writing and for some reason I wasn't able to pull up the last suggested topic of conversation I had heard from Mother Sarah. I had that discerning gnawing feeling that there was something I couldn't recall.

After a short walk, Mother Sarah told me it was time to go to my desk to pick up where we left off. However, after I sat down she didn't speak. Feeling like perhaps I was to *do* something I got a white candle and a stick of rose incense and lit them. I then put on a CD and said a little prayer of thanksgiving and waited. Still nothing. Mother Sarah chose to stay silent.

My comment was, "Mother why are we waiting?" Instead of talking to me, however, she chose to give me clues.

In my office, I had plenty of material to draw the eye for this type of communication. Some had written words on them and some were simply objects. Three times I was shown a capital E which means energy. I assumed there was something amiss with my energy so I got down on the floor and did some stretches. I got up and sat at my desk again. Still nothing was presented. I was about to give up and go do something else when Mother Sarah said, "I am waiting for you to calm down." I was a little surprised at her statement and replied, "I thought I was calm but apparently not."

After a few deep breaths and a short meditation, I was telepathically reminded of the topic concerning why I have had so many men teachers instead of women. "Oh, yes," I said, "now I remember." So I posed my question. "What is the reason for that?" Her answer shocked me, "So you would learn to trust men again." I received the statement like I had received a blow to my body. I felt pain, hurt and despair like I had finally been given a valuable piece of information that I knew belonged to me but I wasn't sure how to integrate it.

"It didn't take but a split second after my disclosure for you to see the truth." Mother Sarah declared. "You have lived in fear of men your entire life. Oh, yes, much of it was on a subtle level, but not so much so that you can't trace the feeling back with every male relationship. It has always come down to not feeling safe in some way, be it on a physical level or perhaps fear of being manipulated mentally—deceived—or even abused emotionally with words or actions meant to inflict emotional pain, or sexually—for the pleasure of the other and not you. There have been feelings of mistrust with almost everyone, including toward your very own ex-husband. So we decided to create relationships with the male members of Telbar to assist you in healing this aspect of trauma. The only man of the entire group that you didn't feel threatened by was your father, Quem.

"You have learned to trust the team members and even Nathanal again. These men are your family members and some have shared lives with you on the Earth plane, some of which may not have been so pleasant. Know that for centuries the Earth and her inhabitants have seen atrocities that even you cannot imagine in this incarnation. There is much healing to come for you and the peoples who are working on their ascension using the theater of the Earth plane.

"At this time, more than at any other in your history, the masses are opening up to the gifts offered to them. We hear the people asking for, allowing and accepting the healing energies that we so eagerly wish to bestow upon them. Blessed are we to have come to this level of consciousness.

"Because you have learned to ask, allow and accept, you are being graced with many teachings that assist you in healing different aspects of yourself. I am your Mother and I love you beyond measure."

✳ ✳ ✳

The following morning began in a rush. I had fallen behind in some of the phone calls I was to make concerning the care of my father. It seemed I was working double time in order to get everything accomplished. I recognized the signs of stress and wanted to relieve my feelings of anxiety and even anger that had erupted when I had to call the same people several times to get something accomplished. I thought back to the weeks I had gone without most of my personal belongings and had lived modestly. Most everyone had not received notice from me of my whereabouts. I guess you could say I was off the grid for the most part—unavailable. My time was relaxed and I had more of it!

After the moving truck delivered my furniture and personal items, all of that simplicity changed; my life got so much more complex. I really would like to have had that simple way again.

One of the things that I was conflicted about was the choice to move my household across the country when I could have just started over. Why was it so important to have this stuff shipped out from Kansas? When we were planning the steps for my move to California, I had told Nathanal that I wanted to sell most of it. I was ready to let go of it. I told Nathanal several times that it was just stuff. But Nathanal had disagreed, even put his foot down and said, "No!" He wouldn't hear any of my reasons for letting go of it. His answer was we didn't have time to sell my things and that they would bring me comfort in the days ahead.

Shipping my belongings to California was expensive. I could have easily used that money to replace my belongings or for something else. However, Nathanal had held his ground and would not be swayed; he stuck to his story that I would be more comfortable with my own things around me—in my home. But as I see it, I feel weighed down.

That day when I went into town to the Post Office, there had been a line, all women, to be waited on. The Post Master on duty was called to the back to check on a package, so there was no one at the counter assisting customers. The women began to chat. Here in Weed, people are much more friendly and will easily begin a conversation. As I waited in silence, I heard one of the women in the back of the line ask another if her house had burned down in the Boles Fire.

The second woman's voice was flat, void of emotion, as she replied, "To the ground."

The woman who had asked said, "Mine too."

Then the woman in front of me began to talk to me. She asked me if my house had burned. I sensed by the way she had shifted her body when the other ladies had said, 'burned down' that she too had lost her home. I answered her by saying, "No, it didn't burn but I was so afraid that it would."

The woman in front of me said, "I lost thirty-eight years of marriage. Everything is gone. My wedding album was burned. I stood across the street and watched it burn." I asked, "Will you rebuild or go somewhere else?"

She shook her head and I saw in her eyes a weariness as she replied, "We are staying with our daughter until we figure out what to do."

Somewhere deep inside of me there was a definite feeling of gratitude that I didn't have my things destroyed. However, there was something else—something more like how come I still had my home and so many others did not? I felt almost like I didn't deserve to have my home. These women certainly didn't deserve to have everything they owned turned to ash in a matter of minutes. People of every social class were affected. There were those who owned their homes while others rented. Some of these people were poor and not able to get up and rebuild on their own while others had good insurance enabling them to take their time and make wise decisions on what to do next.

No matter who they were, it wasn't their choice to have this happen and it had been (still was) a huge shock that all of their material possessions were forever gone and they had no real place to call home any longer.

Before my move here, I had asked Nathanal if it were for my highest good to sell my things Nathanal said, "No." So here I was living in comfort with my own belongings—the belongings that before I felt I had been ready to let go of. None of it made sense. My heart was heavy when I thought of this community and what they had endured—how they were suffering.

"Nakala, this is Nathanal. What has occurred happened on several levels. When we were in Kansas, yes, you said you wanted to sell most of your belongings, only keeping the things that were most dear to you. The rest you could easily sell. The items were not of import to you any longer. We decided to sell a few of the bigger items and keep the rest. I explained that your belongings held energy and would assist you in remaining in a state of peace when you got to California. What I have stated is true. However, when you are a property owner, there is also the aspect of being responsible or being held accountable and this can be looked upon as a burden or looked upon as a gift.

"Let's look at this from another angle. Earlier, you were unable to identify what you were feeling concerning the Boles Fire here in Weed, California."

"You along with everyone else who reside in a human body are a Divine Cosmic Matrix. You are comprised of an emotional, mental, etheric and a physical body. This is the bare bones of how you are built. Through these bodies and the chakras, you are constantly communicating with other humans. In addition, you are communicating with other intelligences and life forms. This is how you are built and what you do.

"You are also empathic and identify with other people's situations and feelings. You are identifying with these people here in Weed. You belong to the Weed community—you live here. These people have suffered a huge trauma and to rebuild isn't their top priority—surviving is. Many walked away penniless. However, they must pick up where they left off and begin anew. Not so easy when the resources seem to be limited.

"Because you are more sensitive and aware, you are more readily picking up on thoughts and emotions of the others who are grief stricken.

"Could any of these people identify their feelings if you were to pose that question to them? Most of them are still in survival mode wrestling with feelings of fight or flight.

"The reason I am discussing this is these people are putting into the ethers what they are thinking and feeling, and it currently it is all a jumbled clutter. You, Miss, are not only receiving these communications from the community but are processing your own feelings as well.

"No, what you have experienced isn't nearly as profound or traumatic, but you were and are a part of this experience. You are going through a grieving period and are to give yourself a bit of room."

I heard my name spoken. It was Mother Sarah. "I have been listening to Nathanal's explanation. I wish to add to the mix. As Nathanal has described earlier, you are a divine cosmic being or matrix created with gifts or abilities that have been long forgotten by your species. There are many of you who are now awakening to these spiritual gifts at the present time. This is why we write the books to assist in easing the way for you who are learning to maneuver through this process.

"In the higher realms, The Boles Fire had been agreed upon by the community as an experience to assist in learning particular lessons."

"Mother," I interrupted, "You make is sound like these people all sat around a table a decided to start that fire—they decided to have their houses burned down."

"No, darling, before you incarnated you agreed to come here for the experience—the lessons that teach you spiritual truths. You agreed to come to the Earth plane knowing full well these types of occurrences happen, and are allowed to happen—the mass consciousness creates these experiences! You will ultimately learn to practice great compassion for your brethren not just have empathy or sympathy for another.

"Now, you were given a teaching via the Element of Fire—the transmutation of energy to begin anew—to create something better with a higher vibration. This is to evolve. That fire was agreed upon and created by the collective community for the experience. No, the majority of people, as of yet, do not understand that the fire was used as a tool to teach them—to assist them to remember that they are beings whose divine essence is LOVE!"

"You know that in times of great distress the greatest good is expressed.

"Over a hundred and thirty homes were destroyed—transmuted into cosmic dust and blown into the ethers. The overseers of the hierarchy are working from an accelerated platform, if you will—not just a few are given the lessons, but hundreds, even thousands receive, as well, as the lessons are expanded outward. There is a spiritual revolution being experienced. There is celebration! The gift of *love* is being expanded on a level unprecedented by this community!

"I am truly pleased to give you this information to assist you in the understanding what is *really* occurring right under your nose."

FOURTEEN

Unexpectedly, one of the ascended masters who had been guiding me over the years, Tulró, showed up here one night. He had not announced himself, merely just began talking to me, (like he had always been here) in his peculiar style that sounded almost southern but not. None of the other guides that I communicate with spoke exactly like Tulró. Then he channeled that foreign language through me—that they say is Pleiadian. I had no idea what was being said at the time. It wasn't long until I figured out that it was Tulró who was speaking.

Even though, over the years, Tulró, through his teachings had managed to push practically every button I had, I was always very happy when he came to visit.

Tulró informed me that he had arrived earlier this morning to assist me with the writings even though I am no longer writing new material. I was in the editing process. So I haven't been entirely sure what he wants me to do.

For the last hour I have been reading and making corrections to my latest book.

When I got to this chapter I heard Tulró interject. "I have been waiting for some time to assist you with the writings." He didn't pause for me to adjust to his energy, just kept speaking as he instructed me, "Start here. This is where I want to write."

He began with, "A few days past you were told by one of the ascended masters that you were to ready yourself to leave this place—this home— in the spring of 2017. You were to begin your travels, extensive, to market your books. Finally, we have goal in mind when you are to have *The Accounts of a Pleiadian Traveler* series complete and ready to be distributed.

"For you, the idea of traveling again under these circumstances is a bit daunting. The master instructed you to begin to lighten your material load as you are guided.

"I say, dear Nakala, you were shocked, mistakenly interpreting the message to mean you would be selling the home and moving on. You reasoned, why else would I be instructed to lighten my load?"

"In the very next transmission, you were instructed to buy framed portraits of three ascended masters and hang them on your office wall. Again you reacted.

"Initially, you saw this as counter-productive as you were just directed to lighten your load. Buy more items? We heard you question this directive for a good while. Logically, what you were being directed to do made no earthly sense.

"Dearest Nakala, the portraits are of high masters and are to be used as a beacon of energy or a point of light. These sacred objects are of a high vibration and are to assist you with keeping the vibration higher in your home and also in assisting you in maintaining your vibration. The pictures are energy and because of who they are will emanate a powerful force of Love.

"I say, Dear One, you are to comply with the directive." I shook my head as I remembered the two distinct messages that were given to me. "Tulró, listen, I have looked around for the portraits of these masters. So far I have not found what would be pleasing to me or to the masters whose pictures will be hanging on my wall.

"Several times I have asked for direct guidance on acquiring these pictures—a way to come by them easily without incurring a great expense. I think I may have insulted the masters by talking about how costly these pictures may be."

"Nakala, be it known there is no judgment. However, your comments directly reflect your frame of mind and your conscious ability to manifest your reality in the physical realm. Think on this Nakala. Perhaps you may procure these portraits in honor of those who serve all for the greater good of humanity."

* * *

Several months had passed and I hadn't heard a word concerning or from my brother, David. My guides had not mentioned him nor had he phoned me or appeared by my side.

However, lately he had been on my mind for several days. It is a peculiar thing that I could go months without his name or face coming into my mind, and then suddenly he was there lingering on the periphery—right on the edge, as if perhaps he wanted to say something or let me know he is still around. It was a subtle energy of sorts and it caused me to pause. There was a chance that he was on someone else's mind and/or heart and I pick up on the thoughts for some reason. So far, I hadn't figured out just how these thoughts came—where they originated from and why. Somehow, I wished he would get on with it, whatever he wanted to say or do.

Maybe David felt it was time that we have another talk and he was working up the nerve to come have his say.

Out of the corner of my eye, I saw the figure of a woman. Her full skirt made a rustling sound as she moved toward me. I didn't know who it was a first…until she spoke. Then I recognized her soft manner. It was Mother Sarah. "Nakala, your brother does desire communications with you. However, he is not strong enough to channel his thoughts to you—over-riding your own personal thoughts. For you to hear him speak, notice when you receive a thought—his name—and sit down at that precise moment and clear yourself of all other activity, all other thought. Then you will be able to hear his message."

"David is ready to clear another level of misaligned energy. Perhaps you can grant him this desire." I wanted clarity so I asked, "Am I receiving his intention? Is that why he keeps coming to the forefront of my mind?"

Mother Sarah paused for a moment as if gathering information. "Yes, he is working with his guides to find the best way to clear all unbeneficial energy. When he is working to clear energy that concerns you, of course his thoughts are on you. When his thoughts are on you, you will undoubtedly receive the communications on some level—depending on your ability. Currently, you are not of the level to know what exactly is being said, but you are of the level to pick up there is a communication of some sort being transmitted."

My thoughts gravitated to how busy I had been lately. To be able to hear my brother's communication and then automatically stop what I was doing seemed unlikely. Since I didn't want to miss this opportunity, though, my solution had been to ask Nathanal to help me recognize when the thought came and make sure that I would sit down to receive—much like a phone call. He had agreed.

Seeing another piece to it, I asked, "Mother, so this is sort of like a telepathic phone call?" She replied, "In this particular instance, David wants to attract and hold your attention but has been unable to thus far. You have been busy with other things in your life.

"I'd like to expand on this idea of telepathic communication or telepathic phone calls, as you coined them; but before I do, I have one more comment to make concerning the thoughts that come to your mind. It has been long noted that when a good friend has you on his or her mind, you may pick up on that thought and vice versa. Once the thoughts begin, one of you will usually pick up the phone and place the call. The first words spoken by the receiver undoubtedly are, 'I was just thinking of calling you!' Thoughts are that powerful. It is quite possible that the two have been playing telepathic phone tag.

"Another part of this is you are picking up on communications that occur between two or more people who are in conversation and your name (or energy) is brought up. It is occurring more and more frequently with you able to detect the emotion behind the conversation: joy, anger, impatience, grief and so on. Thoughts, instantly followed by emotion are very powerful. The more emotion behind the thought the more powerful it becomes. They are magnetic and go where they are sent. Unless, you have turned off that frequency you will receive it consciously or subconsciously.

"Do you recall the teaching you received on tagging people's energy?" Mother Sarah read my thoughts that I had, then continued. "You were warned never to talk negatively about another person. As a child your parents would reprimand you by saying, 'if you can't say anything nice, don't say anything at all.' Your parents on Earth were talking about saying something nice in the other person's presence. I am not only addressing the previous directive but addressing the activity of speaking behind someone's back. Thoughts are the same way. Do not think about another in a negative manner while they are with you or in another locality as they will most assuredly receive them!

"For example: If you notice that a person's work ethic doesn't meet your expectations, you may instantly tag the person's energy or judge them with your thoughts—your opinion! These thoughts go straight to them. It depends on the person's spiritual mastery how the energy will affect them. Is a person able to deflect, possibly even transmute, the energy, not allowing those thoughts and feelings to penetrate his or her field; or is he or she vulnerable to other people's negative energy (critique or judgment), compounding his or hers own feelings of inadequacy and so on?

"In conclusion, the other part of this equation—the energy I speak of is your *very own creation*—you own it; and it will come back to you, affecting you on a very precise level be it positive or negative, it matters not, unless you transmute the energy. This is karma. Always, always speak positively of and to others to consciously uplift them. Positive thoughts are, in turn, a higher frequency and if accepted by the receiver will assist them. Yes, my dear, positive thoughts as well come back to you affecting you as well.

"When you are able to recognize the true essence of love that resides in every living being, it is easy to speak to and of them in a conscientious and loving manner. They are working, just as you, to evolve. They take their experiences, just as you, sorting through them and using them as clues on how to proceed on their life's journey for the highest good.

"Dearest Nakala, it is time I take my leave."

Usually I wrote until 5:00 p.m. With the way Mother phrased her statement I wasn't sure of her true meaning. Immediately, I asked, "What do you mean? Are you leaving for the day? It is still early."

"Nakala, I am called elsewhere. My time with you on this project is finished for now. I bid you farewell."

Stunned that our time had ended so quickly, I scrambled to process her words and stated, "Mother, I thought when you said you were taking the role as master writer, that meant that you would be working with me for a longer period of time. I feel we just began."

"Yes, I know, Dear One. Master writer is merely a term we use that means to be in charge of the writing. When I agreed to step in as master writer and told you as much, I saw within you grandiose visions. However, to write is not my main function. I am Queen of Myra and my responsibilities are vast; I must balance all. Know that I love you and I hold you in my heart always.

"Your father and I will be in the area for an extended stay. We plan to stop in to visit you from time to time."

The feelings of gratitude swelled and I knew that the time I had been allowed would be treasured forever.

During the weekend, Babaró revealed that Stephanó would be arriving on Monday to work with me on this book. I had been surprised because Stephanó is a doctor. Doctors heal people. He is the one who comes to me when I am ill. I questioned if he had time for something as trivial as writing.

Swiftly, Babaró redirected my thought process by saying, "the writing process in not in the least bit trivial." I then had been instructed to assess my choice of words and why I had chosen them in the first place.

My initial thought had been doctors are extremely busy seeing to their many patients and healing them. They are out saving lives. Therefore, they are certainly more important and more in demand than say a writer may be. That is when Babaró decided he would step in to further correct my misguided opinion on the matter.

"Nakala, we are in this together. Yes, Stephanó is busy but so are you. Is his time more valuable than yours? Did God say doctors are more valued than writers? I don't believe I heard that precise lecture. Perhaps I was not in attendance?" I heard him chuckle and knew he was working to ease this lesson.

"Nakala," Babaró continued, "It seems we have a solid hit on yet another core belief that you have held, ever so tightly. Stephanó is indeed an educated master—an ascended master. He works as the family physician for the Pleiadian peoples who are stationed here on the Earth plane. You as daughter of Quem and Sarah are high priority. I am not saying that you are *more important;* you are but one that he assists. Know that when Quem or Sarah directs any of the team members of Telbar to come and assist you, they will and do it as soon as possible.

"When we had the meeting in Myra, Pleiades last year, Stephanó was there. Did you not wonder why he was there—in what capacity?" (This meeting was included in the book, *The Sacred Contract.*) I shrugged my shoulders and paused to think on it. I then answered, "Well, no, at the time, I didn't wonder. Stephanó has been working with me since I first began to receive the communications from the higher realms of light, on a conscious level, telepathic messages from the Pleiadians. He has been here to serve me and in the beginning, I remember, he had been one of the guides who had directed me to either get my journal or my recorder to receive his messages. So, I really didn't think anything was off with his attendance.

"Throughout that trip to Myra, I had been focused on gathering details of the city, the members of Telbar and the meeting in general, all in order that I could write about the experience in more detail.

"Also, at the time, I was just so happy to be with my guides that I had not questioned their exact position in the group of Telbar."

During my conversation with Babaró, I knew that Stephanó was standing to the side, patiently waiting to get on with the writing. But as the conversation with Babaró developed, I decided to get up and look for Stephanó's personal book. I had laid it out a few days ago to record an herbal remedy that he had prescribed for me.

At once, I noticed that Stephanó's book had only a few entries in it. That brought to mind that I have been documenting messages from Stephanó for years. Unfortunately, the majority of his messages were sprinkled throughout my personal journals. I wondered why he, in addition to so many of the other guides, had directed me to create personal books for them; yet most of the time they had chosen to have me write their messages in my personal journals.

Suddenly, I heard Stephanó's voice take on an air of authority as he made his intention clear: "I am ready to begin now."

We exchanged pleasantries and then Stephanó began to dictate his message in earnest. "When you were outdoors conversing with Trent last Friday, (three days past), he openly stated that the weather would turn

Sunday night (Trent is the consciousness or spirit of the cedar tree which lives a few feet outside my back door.)

Any time when you receive information like that please get as many details as possible. You made an assumption that Trent's message meant the weather would turn cold."

"I remembered the message very well, Stephanó. I thought that he meant the weather would become bitterly cold because Trent used the word 'severe.'"

"Yes, that is my purpose in this teaching. You see plainly that you misinterpreted his words—you assumed his meaning. Today—Monday—the winds have picked up considerably—the pine needles have gathered momentum, raining down on your roof like it is hailing. The tall trees sway to and fro like they are performing a major feat to remain standing upright. A front is moving in for certain. The message is there are variables to everything. When you receive any type of message it would be wise to have clear details relayed to you if at all possible.

"Since day one, we have been working with you on clear communications: to ask specific questions so you may receive clear, concise answers that cannot be misconstrued. It is imperative that you do not assume anything. Get direct information. Write it down so you may refer back to it at a later date. As you learn to understand the nuances of particular information, you are to examine it like a detective. Not all is straight-forward or as it *seems* to you."

❋ ❋ ❋

"My name is Stephanó Francisco Akasie. I am an ascended master and the head Akasie family physician. There are many other doctors who are of the higher realms in support of those on the Earth plane. You remember Franklin? He too, works in this capacity. You might say I am employed by the Kingdom of Myra, a United Kingdom sovereign under God. I answer to King Quem and Queen Sarah. Usually, I do not use their official titles as Quem is my brother. This message is merely to support their titles and their import to the Pleiadian Kingdom of Myra.

"There are many of us who have come from the Stars of Pleiades to assist in the evolution of the people of the Earth. We have family evolving in this arena or realm, and it is our desire to serve by tending to their needs when we are allowed to. We work with others here as well. Again, it is a matter of asking, allowing and accepting the gifts from us.

"Nakala, you decided on a higher level to bring in much light during this embodiment—developing a higher more expanded awareness and going into a higher vibratory state. Because of this vow and because you have been and still are highly motivated to go forward, we watch over you more carefully than at any other time.

"When I first began to work with you, there were signs within all levels of your divine cosmic body that indicated you were well on your way to manifest disease on the physical level. We had to work fast to prevent complete collapse of the physical body. You have had several spiritual surgeries since that time. We have worked and continue to do so to get your system working in divine order as Father-Mother God intends.

"Today, I have chosen to speak on this topic because there are several people who have chosen this path, and they too are receiving special care under those such as Franklin and I."

"Because you, Nakala, have been activated and attuned to a specific frequency that gives you the ability to hear our communications, after procedures I may pass on instructions that, if followed, will most assuredly assist you in the healing process.

"There are those who receive this same type of care and are unable to comply with protocol as they are unaware. However, there are thought transmissions and physical symptoms that clearly communicate to the patient that rest is required. Sometimes, the rest is heeded; other times it is ignored. We do what we can. Enough said."

I stopped and thought about his last statement, wondering why someone would be gifted to receive any type of procedure be it on an etheric or physical level without knowing it is going on.

Working to comprehend Stephanó's statement, I asked for clarity. "Stephanó, this really doesn't make sense to me. Why would you perform surgery on anyone who doesn't know they are receiving it?" His reply took me to a whole other level of understanding "It is quite simple," he explained. "Their Higher Self works to continue life in the human form, and the level of awareness of the person will depend on what the Higher

Self wants to do. Oft times, the Higher Self will request procedures to give the Lower Self additional opportunities. Sometimes it works, sometimes it does not. In any case we give it the old college try.

"Stephanó, what happened to the rule to ask, allow, and accept?" Stephanó's answer was, "That is still in place but you see this is on an entirely different level of awareness. When the Higher Self requests a procedure, the Higher Self is working to prolong life in order for the soul to continue his life's journey and to receive more opportunities for learning. I should say the procedure, in itself, is an opportunity to love the human body and listen to its signals by giving it the proper rest.

"Perhaps I give it that it is a *special* circumstance? With a case like yours, you have learned that you are to interface with us directly because you have achieved a higher level of understanding or an expanded level of awareness."

✳ ✳ ✳

"In an entirely different light, I'd like to speak to you of what is occurring in your home. Just yesterday, you completed the organization of your things that arrived just recently from Kansas. The completion of this task brought forth a high state of joy and gratitude not only from you but from us, as well. All of us who have joined with you on this journey are quite pleased that you have come this far.

"Today we continued to direct you to go through some more papers and journals in order for you to reacquaint yourself with the material that you have been given over the years. I am directing your attention to the journals and books that you have spoken of earlier containing downloaded information from different light beings and councils.

"Always you are directed to record transmissions in a particular journal. I will take Babaró as example. He has had you create three different journals for him. Although, most of the time when he dictates a message, he deviates from his journals and has you record the message into your personal journal. This leaves you feeling confused and suspicious that something is amiss. In essence, what you are directed to do does not seem logical. Why is it that you have been guided to created countless books—each one for a specific being, council or endeavor? For you it seems counterproductive—disorganized.

"The communications come from many points of light. In the beginning, we told you that you were being prepared for the messengers that would be traveling the galactic highways and you are. Nakala, you are one of the many scribes chosen to document the scores of messages that come from the higher realms.

"At this moment we are readying you for the many books that you will be channeling for the light beings who wish to serve by contributing to the Earth via the written word.

"You are in training, as it were, building structure by learning to receive data via telepathic communications. There will be a day when it all comes together smoothly and you will see the wisdom of it all."

CHAPTER
SIXTEEN

The weather has *turned* just like Trent predicted. The wind continued to send the seventy to one-hundred foot tall trees into a constant rocking motion. The clouds had become the prominent feature with the sky posing as a light gray back-drop. Mt. Shasta was cloaked in a concentrated layer of fog. It looked like rain was imminent. Clearly, Fall had made its way into northern California.

The rush to get my things in place was over. I felt relaxed and ready to concentrate on writing in peace and solitude.

The times were growing in number when I found myself sitting in a high state of love and gratitude. Intellectually, I knew that I was to get up and produce something tangible, although sometimes I sincerely wondered, what is the point of it all? To move away from the feelings of love and appreciation to do mental tasks such as writing seemed like going backwards—away from the light. I found myself in a quandary: living in a world of third dimensional tasks and objects, doing what I'd call busy-work while I was transitioning to a higher place. I felt like I had each foot in a different dimension.

I knew Stephanó was waiting for me. He was ready to give me his words. Sometimes to settle in and receive was a challenge. It isn't that it was difficult for me to channel because that part wasn't the issue. It was this perpetual feeling that overpowered me. I kept turning around to look out the backdoor to see the trees. The beauty and wonder of it all distracted me, and for writers that isn't a good thing.

Just then Stephanó channeled a breath through me and said, "Nakala, relax." He continued to channel deep breaths through me, filling my lungs with rich oxygen. I felt my vibration rise and I felt the tears threaten to spill over. That day I had felt like crying every time I turned around. Then Stephanó asked me, "Are you ready to begin?" Unable to speak, I nodded my head, yes.

"Good," Stephanó said "It is my pleasure to bring to you these words… these teachings. When a weather systems moves, in the atmospheric pressure changes."

"I want to give you this lesson because it is important that you understand that first, you are in a higher elevation than you are accustomed to. Second, you are living in a vortex. Three, a weather system has moved in.

"This morning when you checked the thermometer outdoors, it read 60 degrees instead of 39 degrees. For the last three weeks, every night the temperature has dipped below the 40 degree mark. Suddenly, the wind moved in and with it the clouds. The temperature has risen considerably indicating a huge shift in the weather pattern.

"You have an emotional body, Nakala. When pressures in the weather system change, you feel it emotionally. (Presently, your emotional body is expanded.) This is why you feel like crying. This is why the gratitude over-rides. This is why you do not feel like doing anything on the physical level. Your bodies are not aligned properly at this moment."

Immediately, I used the technique that I had learned to align my bodies hoping that I would feel instant results. On an intellectual level, just going through the steps eased some of my discomfort. Thinking Stephanó had concluded his teaching I said, "Thank you, for explaining this to me."

"I am not finished just yet." Stephanó said. "You are living in the mountains, which is a higher altitude. In addition, you are living on the outer perimeter of a major vortex. All of these factors amplify any emotion. If you are feeling particularly grateful or sad, then the conditions, I stated beforehand, will intensify your feelings, causing you to feel weepy. In addition, when a weather system moves in on top of these other factors, you again have an exorbitant magnification of energy.

"We are pleased that you are in a place that will increase your emotions because it is a great teaching for you. But it doesn't end there. Your thoughts are magnified as well. You have noticed that you are manifesting your desires more quickly here. The energy is such that it is assisting you in moving forward toward your goals of completing your sacred contract in this embodiment and onward to the fifth dimension.

"Father-Mother God has created everything in your world and beyond, all in order to assist you in your steps in evolution, enabling you the ability to hold more of the cosmic light—an expansion of energy and consciousness. Nakala, when you view everything in your day in this manner, you are elevated to a higher perspective, your trip to the fifth dimension is accomplished with ease and grace, and it is a more enjoyable experience. May I add that your trip to the fifth dimension may even be considered fun?"

"Much of the human race desires to move into the fifth dimension. However, they don't understand that *every single* experience is designed to be a life lesson—an opportunity to learn to love all of creation. This means to see the perfection of God's creation.

"I am a doctor—a scientist and I find great pleasure and joy in examining God's creation. I don't just look at what I can see on the surface, I look deep within and see the workings of that creation. Take the cedar tree, Trent, who resides nearby. Trent is not merely a giant column of fibrous tissue or wood with branches reaching upward and outward with a magnificent root system, as well. Trent is a life form—a consciousness that is alive and well. He is connected to all other life forms in nature. Oh, but it goes far beyond, as Trent is of the Nature Kingdom and was created to complement the humans during their sojourn on Earth. Trent is very much connected to you as well. Believe it or not he, along with the entire Nature Kingdom, is in service to you. You just haven't realized that he is here for this specific reason.

"The implications of my previous statement are incredible indeed. Think on it and see if you view any life form the same again. Each life form has been created to complement the others, making a whole. Beautiful it is."

Stephanó paused long enough for me to think the teaching was complete; then I heard Stephanó interject, "No, there is more I would like to share with you.

"Nakala, you have had literally hundreds of human embodiments on this Earth. Trent, as well, has incarnated over and over again on this

Earth. With each embodiment both you and Trent are learning more and expanding your consciousness.

"Earlier in this text you were given a teaching on the transmutation of energy via fire. That particular teaching was a difficult one because the image of fire ravishing the trees had an adverse sensory impact—it haunted you. In fact, the image of trees being consumed by the flames has haunted you more than the houses turning to ash on Angel Hill. Why do you suppose that is?"

Stephanó's question had caused an instantaneous upheaval of emotion. Sensing a shift in the way I perceived things, I said, "It isn't that I don't empathize or sympathize with the people. They too were tormented, uprooted, and grief-stricken by the consequences of the fire. However, they were able to flee, in some capacity, from the flames. The houses are just houses and can easily be re-built. The trees and plants, however, are rooted deeply in the earth, making it impossible for them to move away from any danger. When I think of the forests that are senselessly burned for reasons unknown, I literally feel physical pain."

"Yes, it is a great loss when one loses their physicality—a way to evolve using the Earth as the schoolroom. However, you are to remember that you are eternal beings and perhaps the passing or the circumstances behind it is part of the lesson.

"So instead of going into a grief-stricken state, think on this: Everything you experience is collected and used for further expansion, *everything!*

"I believe that with this newly acquired knowledge you will not allow yourself to be driven to the depths of despair when a life form passes from its earthy body, but instead you will rejoice in the lessons that have given the experience necessary to gain a higher level of wisdom and freedom."

"Stephanó," I began, "From what you have said, I really think that I will be able to be grateful for the opportunity to have the experience here on Earth instead of dwelling on how unfair it may be to leave at any given time and for whatever reason."

"You know, Nakala, you have come here to engage and expand yourself with more of God's creation. I look at it like this: You have come here to California because you are ready to have this experience—the occasion to live in the glorious mountains during this lifetime—to experience first-hand the senses to build on your tactile memory. In other words, you are learning in a new and stimulating ecosystem.

"Books, movies, and the like engage you and may transport you fairly well to how it feels to experience any given place by evoking the senses on a particular level. However, they are temporary and a far cry from actually living in the physical location.

"Perhaps these mediums are but to give you a small taste—to entice you a bit to move to another classroom so you will partake *fully* with your physical senses. Unless, you engage yourself physically you will not have the complete understanding or encounter. To sum it up, you are here to get the full impact of what it is like to physically live—to express yourself in this climate and this terrain with this group of souls."

I was beginning to understand that part of why I had moved to California was my Higher Self wanted me to be in a different environment/classroom to expand my consciousness. I can look at it like this—Kansas, while it had been a spectacular painting, was merely a foundation of sorts or a canvas. For a while I lived in that painting or made each stroke of the brush. With each precise and intentional stroke, I had personally added the color and texture of the scene, creating my experience that aided in the development of my life throughout my lessons. With my thoughts, feelings and actions I had created my painting—my life. That was the reality I had chosen to create. For me, the Kansas painting had been complete. Perhaps I just wasn't gaining anything of significance from it any longer. I had enjoyed it for the duration and now I was complete. In order to be stimulated on a different level, I had been prompted to come to California with a blank canvas and begin a new painting—a new life.

* * *

Three weeks ago I had taken a class at the Marble Rim Gallery to learn to make pine needle baskets. I wasn't able to finish mine during the allotted time. Because the instructor saw my sincere interest, at a later date he had called me up and invited me out again. But that wasn't really the lesson. When I received the call I had been thrilled! However, the day that he had available to help me had conflicted with a specific time I had agreed to write with Stephanó. Truly, I felt I didn't have a choice in the matter.

I had made a previous commitment with Stephanó; and, well, to break an engagement with an ascended master…I didn't think so!

However, my heart was speaking clearly. My greatest desire had been to go work on my basket! I am an artist and to create something pleasing gives me joy. My heart was singing at the opportunity but my mind was weighed down with thoughts of my previous commitment. Clearly, I felt it would not be prudent to break it.

Nathanal saw my perceived dilemma and openly suggested that I ask Stephanó to change dates. Silently, I felt a tinge of dread but my response had been, "It couldn't hurt." I asked Nathanal to notify Stephanó that I'd like to talk to him. Nathanal curtly put the ball in my court by saying, "You do it."

Even though I had had the teaching that my time was as valuable as Stephanó's, I still had remained fixed on my belief. In my mind, Stephanó was tremendously busy and for him to come work with me on the writing was more than I could ever ask for. To ask him to change dates would cause him to have to rearrange his schedule, which I had promptly but erroneously concluded would be a major ordeal. Nathanal had, in his way, challenged me; so I decided to give it a try.

Telepathically, I called out, "Stephanó." No answer. I called out another time; this time I added, "Stephanó, I'd like to talk with you." Still there wasn't an answer. At the time I felt there was nothing more I could do.

I went back to my task at hand and forgot my query. Approximately ten minutes later Stephanó said, "This is Stephanó, what is it you need?" I explained the situation, feeling guilty with every word. I figured he would not be able to switch around his schedule; so when he said, "Of course we can change days," I was more than pleasantly surprised. But once again feelings of guilt emerged—this time because I had assumed that Stephanó would not be able or willing to change his schedule for me. My belief had been that doctors are too important and busy to have to change around their lives for people like me.

So imagine my dismay when I woke up the next morning to find Stephanó assisting me with getting around for the day. Something deep inside of me rumbled with the new persona that Stephanó was presenting. I mentally argued with myself and with Stephanó that what he was doing was incorrect. This new tactic had thrown me off-kilter. I couldn't—wouldn't accept his help. Because of my belief that I am inferior to people who have demanding schedules (like more important things to do). I said, "Stephanó you should go. I am sure you have other things way more important this morning to do than hanging out with me."

His tone was easy to read as his emotions had come to the surface. He stated, "Nakala I am a person just like you are in the sense that I like to do many different things. I have family—you are my family. To be balanced, people engage in a variety of activities and conversations with many different types of people.

"You think my only function is to take care of people who are ill?" Stephanó paused and then continued as his voice became stronger—infused with the energy of power and authority, "Not at all! You do remember, don't you, that meeting that we both attended last year in the Kingdom of Myra before the coronation? I sat at the table alongside of the other members of Telbar. This group, Telbar was formed specifically by members of the Akasie who desire to assist you throughout your journey on Earth, taking you to the fifth dimension. I am such one person. Yes, I serve as your personal doctor, but we are family and it brings me great joy to spend time with you.

"Think on this: as a writer and channel would *you* like to occupy yourself only with other writers and talk *only* about your work? Would *you* like to *always* be in discussion with others on channeling? Would *you* always want to be in service as a channel, never being with your family? Possibly, just possibly, you hold other interests. It is quite probable that you would not only like to involve yourself in other endeavors but would highly benefit from them, as well.

"My point being, as a balanced person, you have many interests. I do as well. I am an ascended master. Yes, I have many responsibilities. Do you think that as an ascended master I only want to work?

"We, the masters, are here to serve, and this brings us much joy: but that is only a part of our lives.

"You have known me for some time and received many communications from me over the years. But I ask you, do you truly know me?"

"Stephanó," I began, "I felt that you were always here on business. I didn't feel like you were here to visit…ever."

"Well, let me say this. As one of your teachers, we have been extremely focused in getting you to this place—not just California but this place where you have a better understanding of your purpose and ours, as well. You have come to this place and now our intent is to break down any remaining obstructions to further enhance healing and expansion of all.

"It is time that you get to know your Pleiadian family." Then he paused before he put the question to me—for me to assess, "Don't you think it is time you get to know your Pleiadian family?"

I felt my heart expand, but at the same time the feelings of sadness erupted and then came an undercurrent of the inexplicable notion of me being small as I explained my side, "I tried to get to know you all a long time ago…I gave up. I was always getting messages to teach me things. So you are saying it is time that you will let me in?" Stephanó gave me a single nod as he replied, "Yes, the time has come."

CHAPTER
SEVENTEEN

The High Priest of Telos, Adama, began his transmission by saying, "Many days have passed since our last communication. I came to you in the year of 2012 to invite you to come visit our glorious mountain. (The message was given telepathically.) As it turned out life got in the way and it was 2014 before you were able to come here.

I have kept my eye on you since you first learned on a conscious level of my existence—our existence—as I knew that the time was near for us to serve together as a team. (Telos is the city located inside of Mt. Shasta. The people are of Lemurian descent.)

Always, you have been in my prayers. So you see I did not turn away because you did not arrive the moment that I would have liked." (Here Adama was referring to the fact that there were no more communications from him since the date of his invitation.)

"The days pass swiftly because you have goals that intrinsically you feel must be met. You, on a higher level of awareness, have an awareness that your inner promptings have quickened. There is an inner stirring—drive—to accomplish in not only the physical realm, but the higher realms, as well. Your desire to reach a particular destination has sped up your energy on all levels of your being. This creates a vortex of sorts—a spinning of energy speeding up time or so it seems.

"I remind you to remain steadfast to your promise—your sacred contract—but on a conscious level you are to stay present—be in the moment fully, allowing yourself to savor each experience."

For me to have Adama finally channeling the above message seemed like a long-awaited wish that had finally been granted. I was grateful, yet I was full of feelings of excitement—expectation that bordered anxiety. I had wanted to reconnect, even live with the people of Telos for such a long time. A part of me had felt like by moving here to California, I had finally come home—to pick up where I had left off so long ago.

Before the prophetic cataclysmic event of the sinking of the Continent of Lemuria, I had been a citizen of that community, Lemuria, and a high priestess. The intimate details of that long-ago life remained elusive— hidden in a shroud of mystery. Yet, deep in my heart, there remained a strong sense of connection, a bond if you will, with these people who are a definitive part of my soul family.

During a past life retrieval to assist me in healing, I was given a tiny shred of evidence that yes, I had been part of the Lemurian race— these people.

The memory invoked hadn't been a pleasant one. Yet it was evidence— a confirmation that what I felt in my heart concerning the Lemurians and Mt. Shasta had been genuine.

The memory stirred was a projection of sorts—like a scene being viewed in a movie. I, with a small group of woman had been attempting to escape the unavoidable. We had been set in a small rowboat pitted against the horrific winds and the unsurmountable sea that had rushed in like a tidal wave conclusively sucking us under into an abyss of blackness.

Before we perished into the void, we had huddled together for warmth as much as for the comfort we shared with another. We prayed to God for mercy—to be saved. The ocean waves were fierce and the night moonless. The torrential rains and the invincible waves sent our bodies far out into the sea where we had been finally laid to rest granting us peace and serenity. During that time, my aim had been to offer up my prayers to God for mercy, setting aside my own feelings of distress to calm the fears of a few others.

Without pause, I heard Adama emphatically state, "We will not get into that, as it is finished. You were given—shown this tiny piece of this one past life when Lemuria sank to assist you in expediting your healing process—in resetting yourself to the still-point. Allow me to continue. The still-point is a place you are to go to in meditation and ultimately, with dedication you will learn to access this state of being instantly. Later, in your development, you will *be* in this place always no matter the circumstance."

"Adama, I think I have heard this term before: the still-point."

But before I received any clarification, I began to feel sick. My head hurt and my stomach churned…I was nauseous and thought I might lose my lunch. I could not continue writing, so I asked what I should do to ease my discomfort. I felt this intense energy that had to somehow be released. Immediately someone directed me to lie down on the floor.

I didn't understand why I felt so badly. It had come on so swiftly. The crux of the matter was I rarely feel ill. As I lay there on the floor for a few minutes, I contemplated this bizarre situation and then, suddenly, without explanation I was directed to rise and go outdoors.

To me, the fact that it was raining didn't matter. The fresh, cool, damp air was helping me to release the energy when the thought occurred to me that it might be Adama's energy that I had reacted to.

While I was still outdoors, Adama began to speak to me again. I felt better, so I came back inside to type his words. "As I was saying," Adama picked up where he had left off, "I am channeling these words. Nevertheless, you feel my radiation. I am connected to you energetically. I must be vigilant in maintaining a vibration that will not be uncomfortable for you. This is the reason why I have stated, out-right, through my appointed messengers that few will be invited inside the mountain to visit our beautiful city, Telos. Those who are invited will not be allowed to stay long. You are not ready to be subjected to this high level of energy. I allowed you to feel this frequency to remind you, your time to live with us has not come. Rest assured your day is coming. Every day you are getting closer to achieving the mastery of love, which is stillness or the still-point.

"Nakala, you have asked us for assistance with growing your own food. Sakeem, who has been stationed for some time in Telos, is an extension of us—he represents us. He has joined your team and he is to assist you in many areas. I know, as well as your team knows, you have a great desire to properly care for your physical body.

"In order to appropriately support and balance your physical body, one of the things you must give it is the highest nutrition possible. You, as well as many others, are now shifting your template to consume fresh vegetables, fruits, nuts and grains instead of processed products. I purposely used the term "products" to bring you to a better understanding that these items that are prepackaged for your *convenience* are not actually what we would identify as healthy or even as food. Fresh produce straight from the garden is what the physical body craves and most assuredly deserves.

"Another in the physical will come your way to assist you in the physical makings of your new vegetable garden."

Looking out my back door, at my tiny three and a half by fifteen feet area, I speculated how growing my own food would be accomplished. I didn't believe it to be nearly large enough to grow what I required to thrive.

"Nakala," Adama pointed out, "you have a small area, but you can grow what you want." However, logically, I saw challenges ahead of me. *How would I get all of my beloved vegetables to grow on this tiny patch of earth?* In addition, there was also the matter of wildlife here that had a habit of sauntering through the area and nibbling on whatever was available.

"Adama, I know there are techniques to accommodate nature and animals, but I haven't been taught how. Will Sakeem or someone else teach me these things?" "Of course," Adama answered quickly as if it were all preplanned—decided upon. "You will be directed by the correct guides when the time is in alignment to do so.

"Let's move on, shall we?

"Nakala, you have been instructed to walk the paths of Mt. Shasta to connect with the mountain's energy as well as ours. This activity will greatly expand and quicken your vibration. In order to achieve your goals going to the fifth dimension and join us, this is *the* one activity that will assist you the most at this time. There are many other areas that you can concentrate your efforts upon, as well, to expand your consciousness and your vibration, but to physically and energetically *be* with the mountain is the main priority."

My thoughts went directly to the fact that winter was fast approaching. The higher one goes in elevation, the more unpredictable the weather is. I wondered if he meant I should do these walks when the weather was cold, so I asked for clarification. "Adama, the weather is shifting. Winter is near and the rains have arrived. The road closes for the winter at Bunny Flat in one week."

I was relieved to hear Adama say, "Nakala, it is not wise for you to travel on days like these. The fog alone is visually impairing. However, you listen to your guides, correct? When your guides direct you to go to the mountain, go. With them you are always safe."

Adama had read my thoughts and commented, "I believe you feel that the time isn't convenient for you to begin these walks. Perhaps you feel the writings overshadow any expeditions on the mountain?"

I didn't answer right away. I felt, on a personal note, as if I were making excuses for not going to the mountain for these walks. "Okay," I said as if the word would somehow lengthen the time I had to respond. "Adama, every moment of everyday is full. I do not have much time for myself. To add another task, no matter how wonderful it sounds (at this moment walking on an extreme incline in the mud, snow and cold did not sound that great to me). I feel over-taxed. I do not know how to add anything else to my schedule.

"I felt a sense of guilt, as though perhaps what I was saying was a poorly executed excuse. But honestly, I knew that I am still adjusting to the area, my new home, the energy of the place. I could sure use some help managing my days. My guides were assisting me, but it was *I* who was doing all of the physical labor. I was balancing my life, home and work by myself. Some days the load felt incredibly heavy.

"That isn't all of it. It is *how* I feel when I travel up the mountain. I feel utterly alone but at the same time it is as if someone is watching me. I don't feel entirely comfortable or even safe."

I continued, "Adama, it isn't my intention to complain or make excuses why I am not following your guidance although that is exactly what it sounds like I am doing. It isn't going to help for me to say, 'Okay, Adama, I'll get right on it' and then "conveniently" forget your advice. I have to be honest here. Somehow, I must balance my life. Somehow, I thought, with coming here to California my life would get simpler and I would have more time to spend in nature, but so far it hasn't."

"Nakala, I know at this moment you feel frustrated. You are currently making shifts in your daily regimen in order for you to have more time to work on your spiritual path. This is good that you have spoken so openly. How else are you going to go forward unless you acknowledge what troubles you?

"On the Earth's surface one of the main issues is learning to balance one's life. That is to have the proper focus and know what activity is the correct priority in one's life in any given moment. A fair number of people on the surface are enmeshed in the endeavor to earn the almighty dollar. They must eat and have shelter in order to survive. You must have a way to pay for these things."

I knew that what Adama was about to give me was huge, and suddenly I felt meek and insecure—not up to the task to channel his message with absolute integrity. After that thought, several deep breaths were channeled through me to ease my anxiety.

"As I was saying," Adama continued. "The people are caught up in a never-ending cycle of earning enough income to pay for their *physical needs.* Because so much energy is allotted for the physical, there is little energy remaining not only for working on their sacred path but to even realize that they have a sacred path! In addition, little attention is placed upon maintaining mental and emotional health. You have an etheric body, as well, that requires attention. So you see there is much to contend with as you continue your journey on the Earth. By the time you take care of your basic needs there is little energy remaining for spiritual growth or even the time that it takes to nurture yourself by loving yourself and doing what makes your heart sing. Ah, the people have grown so far away from their true selves, their essence—love.

"People in general have been hypnotized. They rise from their night's sleep (if they are able to sleep that is), go to work, (most of time these people work for the money not for the love of it). Then they go home watch TV, fill their stomachs with fast food, do a few basic things then go to bed. Where is the joy?

"Nakala, you see my words are filled to overflowing with negativity. I apologize here. Our words in this context are for teaching purposes, not meant to judge. But the truth of the matter must be faced in order to change it! People must see what is occurring before they may seek a higher order, follow it, and make it their own.

"Now, change takes courage, determination and dedication. Why, just to change your diets by reintroducing vegetables may be quite the challenge.

"The masses will find they must research to learn what is best for them. What is priority? Do they set out to learn to shop differently or perhaps learn to grow their own food? Moreover, are they to prepare their foods more healthily? These are only steps.

"For you, personally, these steps have taken years and you are still incorporating the changes needed to go the distance. As individuals and as a collective, you continue to go forward and evolve.

"Our people of Telos keep you in our prayers. We hold you in love and we offer our assistance to you. Should you decide you would like assistance on a more tangible level we will certainly review the request, discerning in what way we may assist for the highest good.

"On another note, Nakala, this is why you are here—to broadcast our existence through your voice and the writings to educate people that we are here to assist by giving forth our wisdom and love through the messages.

"We have been stationed under the surface of Mt. Shasta for thousands of years. It is a beautiful place and we love it here. We are to join with you soon, resurface and teach you many of our ways. But until that time arrives we will continue to move forward as we have by channeling our messages and, yes, coming to visit on the surface on occasion. This is to allow you to reacquaint yourself with us…our wisdom and our energy.

"There are those on the surface who have already learned the disciplines, shifting easily to the fifth dimension. You are one who is working toward this goal.

"One of the very first lessons you are to master in order to balance yourself must be to set your priorities—make time to learn of God's truths and practice them! One of most basic concepts is The Law of Attraction—to understand, be they positive, neutral or negative, your thoughts and feelings attract the same, thus creating your reality.

"In order to live a life of love, abundance, and grace people must grasp this very concept, understanding that they are transmitting this energy to the universe in the first place. Practice the Law of Attraction by staying focused on the positive. If you slip by going into the negative, so be it. Do not compound the energy by rehashing it. Keep practicing until you master this. You can look at this lesson like you are mastering any desired skill—it takes dedication, patience and practice for anything to be mastered. ~Yours, Adama"

After Adama had gone, Babaró informed me that Adama would be returning the next day to continue his transmission. I looked at the clock as I rushed through my chores, all the while wondering how I would possibly get it all finished before his arrival.

As I was sitting at the kitchen table staring at my plate that was overflowing with food, I told Samuel Paul (he had been assisting me with preparing my breakfast and filling my plate), that he had served me much too much food. He said in his matter of fact voice, "You are not getting enough calories or the proper nutrients." Unintentionally, I snapped at him and said, "I can't get it all in one meal! I can't even eat this much."

Unruffled, Samuel Paul continued, "What you do not eat, throw out." Thinking back to the countless times I had been instructed—ordered—by my biological parents to clean my plate, I countered, "That seems a bit wasteful to me, Samuel Paul."

"Nakala, the food has been prepared. Each day it sits in the refrigerator, the lower the vibration goes. What you do not eat today, discard."

Before I took a bite of my food, I gave thanks—all the while stewing at not having my chores finished before Adama was to arrive. Then suddenly, for no logical reason, I slowed down my eating and my thoughts shifted. I no longer felt rushed but instead I felt relaxed and knew everything was in perfect order. It was as if nothing mattered except my meal, and I knew that Adama would be available when I sat down to write.

As if I were moving in slow motion, I finished my breakfast; then I moved on to finish preparations for my next meal by chopping and filling my crock pot with fresh vegetables for a nice soup, then I cleaned up the dishes. It all seemed rather odd...I felt rather odd.

Before I sat down to write at my desk, I was directed to sit down on the couch to receive words that I believed to be of a personal nature (not to be shared) from Adama. After that was complete I moved to the adjoining room—my office.

It was time to sit down at my computer; however, no words were offered by any of the beings of light. I waited. Then a wonderful feeling of love washed over me and my vibration quickened. Adama said, "Go into the kitchen and get yourself a cup of tea, not a pot, just one cup... take care of your personal needs as well. Your parents, Quem and Sarah, wish to speak to me. I will call you when I am ready for you."

I did as directed. It was just a few minutes later when I heard my name called, letting me know Adama was ready to begin.

Adama began by saying, "I have specific information for you before we get back to the teachings. Your father, Quem, and mother, Sarah, have advised me of an upcoming event. They are departing Sunday afternoon to return to Pleiades. With this they have asked me, personally, if I might keep in touch with you and perhaps continue the writings to a certain degree.

"It has been my intention all along to work with you to write and distribute the timely messages that are contributing to the ascension. I would very much consider it an honor if you would join me in this endeavor.

My heart felt like it would burst open as I answered, "I really would like this." Then Adama unexpectedly directed me to retrieve his personal journal and type the message he had given me while I sat in the living room just a few moments earlier.

I got his journal out and opened it to the last transmission.

"Father Adama, thank you for coming."

"Yes," Adama opened with, "I am desiring greatly to write a passage in your upcoming book, *In the Light of Day.*" (This book)

"Is that to happen today?"

"Yes, but beforehand, I have specific words for you.

"I hear your cries in the night, Nakala, to join with us, your Lemurian family. You believe, perhaps, we can assist you to learn to grow produce teaming with nutrition and high in life force. You also desire us to share with you recipes—the ways to prepare said produce for your highest good. In Telos, we only partake in fresh vegetables, fruits, seeds, nuts and grains. We do not prepare our food by cooking it, which kills the life force. The life force is what you require in order to stay vibrant, youthful and healthy—alive in your physical body.

"You are with strong focus and want to go forward. You understand to take care of your physical body is key to remaining intact—continuing on with your purpose on Earth without the interruption of shedding the flesh time and time again. To carry on with the same flesh body hastens the process of your evolutionary mastery. In other words, you wish to continue on—to build momentum and attain great heights of Light and Love in your present incarnation—physical body.

"All is well. The Masters, Archangels and the Brotherhood of Light— MANY are beside you lifting you up, assisting you to achieve.

"Know you will be given proper information and guidance in order to carry on with the physical vehicle you presently use for many years to come. Indeed!

"Now, let us step into the next room. I will give forth unto you the gift— to share with your brothers and sisters who reside on the Earth plane."

I didn't get up as Adama had instructed. Instead, I questioned Adama about using me as a channel as I had heard at least one other time that he would only use one channel.

"Nakala, in some respects one channel would be most pleasing. However, I have come to you, and I shall work with you to further our cause. Perhaps the statement made was an assumption or perhaps truth at that particular moment. I am to teach many—the word must travel outward. I work with many. I channel communications to *many*.

"You have presented yourself to be in service. I have presented myself, as well, in service. We are United as One.

"Nary will there be only one to reach the masses—there are Masters all over the world and beyond who channel in order to assist in evolution.

Think on it. Jesus channels through multitudes. Why would I limit the opportunity to share God's Truth?

"Our time draws nigh to join our brethren on the surface. Please allow yourself to embrace this modality of reaching the masses. ~In Peace, Adama"

At that moment, Adama said, "Let's take a break. I'll return in thirty minutes."

It was nice to get up and do a few things—move. The sun had broken through the rain-filled clouds. Again the sky was clear blue.

As I felt Adama's presence once again shift my vibration, I surrendered to the stillness. My mind emptied of all thought and truly I wanted to remain that way forever—completely relaxed; void of all the thoughts that almost always swirl and collide in my mind. The feeling was pure peace.

CHAPTER
NINETEEN

Summer was nearing its final moments on stage. I had been here in California for two months now. I felt like I had already begun to take the beauty that surrounds me for granted.

The last two days we had received a steady, slow-soaking rain. The following morning when I woke up from a deep sleep, it was still dark. I got up anyway. In the moonlight, I saw the mist hanging, suspended, and truly felt like this place was a magical wonderland. Still, I had settled in and the newness didn't affect me like it had in the beginning. For that I grieved: If only I could hang on to the excitement and treasure every moment as if it were the very first time—never before experienced.

I concluded from this experience that I had become accustomed to being fed stimulating data via the senses to remain in a high state of gratitude. This didn't seem like it should be correct. I thought I should be able to remain in a high state of gratitude no matter where I was or what I was doing.

I felt a shift in energy and knew that Adama was ready to begin his teaching. "If you were in a continual state of high gratitude, you would not experience the other emotions. You have been created to feel many levels of energy, one being appreciation and gratitude." Adama paused, allowing the meaning of his statement to sink in. His initial message triggered a memory that I had heard as a child—an analogy of the mountains (the highs) and the valleys (lows). We have highs and lows during our lives. If we only had the highs we would not be aware that they were highs. But then I wondered if it matters. If you are on top of the mountain, does it matter if you actually experience the valley or the lows?

"I believe," Adama resumed, "that you must experience the vast array of emotions in order to learn. Where you are now, collectively, is conducive to achieving control over your thoughts and emotions. This means have an experience, find the good in it, and be grateful for it.

"Currently, many of the people still look for what is wrong, what they don't like—finding fault. This is judgment and one of the lessons you are mastering. May I include that if you did not experience the lows you would not appreciate, in the way you do, the highs or even the states of neutrality.

"God has created the physical body for you, a spiritual being, to have physical experiences or exchanges with other beings in physical bodies; and yes this includes adversity—challenges. In the physical realm, you are learning mastery over the lower desires—thoughts and emotions. As I said before, a great number of people continue to allow their selves to be swayed, entranced, if you will, by the outer influences instead of listening to their hearts. Our aim is to teach through these types of messages that you are fully capable to go forward and learn the art of self-control.

"I am a spokesman for the Telosian people, Nakala. To work with people, such as you, is my function. You look at the duties of priests in your communities and you will know that we are here to connect people, uplift in times of need, and to teach the gospel—word—God's Truth. This is my purpose.

"It is time to put down the paper for today. Your energy wanes. Honor yourself, Nakala." I glanced at the clock and saw we were stopping an hour earlier than planned. Quickly, I assessed my energy and knew that Adama was correct and said, "Well, I am ready to quit. Thank you, Adama."

CHAPTER
TWENTY

With the morning sunrise came the promise of a *special day*. Babaró told me earlier than usual that it was time to make myself available to write. However, before I sat down at the computer, I went into the kitchen and made myself a pot of jasmine tea. The room felt a little chilly even though I had put on a sweater. Hot tea sounded nice.

As I was heating my water, I reflected on the last few days. For me to receive Adama and take dictation from him had been for me unusual, and I wondered if he would come again.

I made myself comfortable at my computer and waited for Babaró to begin. He did not. Instead he directed me to look at the spines of two books. First, he showed me the word "shift" then the word "energy". Babaró wanted me to go into gratitude for the teachings that I had received and would be receiving. After I said my prayers, Babaró said, "Thank you, Nakala. Now we are to begin."

Babaró opened his dictation by saying, "I want to speak on the departure of your Mother and Father this past Sunday. However, before I do, I want to comment on our practice. I would like to make it clear to the reader how we work with you.

"We have set up a schedule to write together. We are extremely organized in our ways. It is because of this that we are able to accomplish our goals. Each day we work on certain tasks, but we balance those tasks with other endeavors so as not to overwhelm or disregard balance of your overall self.

"Nakala, because of your recent move here to California, which entailed much of your time, you are still adjusting and creating the segments of your days—what suits you best. Soon all will flow like clockwork. Yet there will be times of flexibility—spontaneity. This is so you do not become bored and burn out.

"I get back to it. Your mother, Sarah and father, Quem have made it habit to come to you each Sunday morning at 9:00 am. You expect—cherish—their arrival, this sacred time with them. It has been a little different these past few weeks as they have been staying at your home—using it as their home-base.

"Although, these maneuvers don't always hold true, you have noticed they often leave during the day and return home in the evening. Your parents are members of various councils and of the Galactic Federation. They are Emissaries of Light—peacemakers—and as they serve in this capacity they must themselves be available to exchange ideas and possibly assist on some level with endeavors or appoint the appropriate people to assist. This gives you an idea of their function.

"Nakala, the other evening, you saw another side of your parents that delighted you greatly. They announced that they were going out for the evening—just the two of them to have fun! You asked what they were going to do and Quem said, "Go dancing and then perhaps to a movie!" You heard excitement in his voice. You were in awe of his energy level—dancing *and* a movie?"

I shook my head in awe because there is no way I would do both things in one night. One activity a day or even a week is more than plenty for me.

"Yes," Babaró said, "well, when your parents go out, they go out!

"Sunday rolled around and you sat with them giving thanks for all the blessings that you are given. I also had been there during your time together. At one point, you decided you wanted to get in the car and drive up Mt. Shasta even though you knew that your parents were due to leave at noon sharp. But when you asked them about it, they showed that they were excited about the idea and said, "Yes! They could easily abort their pick-up location and enter their new coordinates.""

As they had talked about changing their plans, I had looked at the clock several times to estimate if there would enough time to drive up the mountain, spend some time and then get back home before their flight. For some reason I had trouble shifting to this idea that they could just change where the shuttle would pick them up. They held firm saying, "It does not matter. The shuttle will pick us up wherever we tell them to."

Quickly I had changed into some warmer clothes and we headed south on Highway 5 toward Mt. Shasta City. On the drive up the mountain, I wondered if the road would be closed at the gate at Bunny Flat since it had snowed. We still had one week before they officially closed the road beyond Bunny Flat for the season. Babaró had assured me that the road remained open.

The higher we traveled up the mountain, the colder it became. I stopped at Bunny Flat for a potty break.

As I pulled into a space, I had noticed a couple with their Labrador retriever getting ready to take a hike when Mother Sarah unexpectedly announced that they would be getting out to take a walk before the shuttle picked them up. (They thought a walk would be wonderful before their flight.)

With that announcement, a distinctive feeling had overshadowed my once jovial mood—one of sadness that was on the borderline of despair. At the same time, I was distinctly aware of my emotions and purposefully worked to remain detached. I just didn't want them to leave…ever.

However, we went through the motions and said our good-byes and they got out of the car. I so wanted to be strong and just say, "I'll talk to you later," but was unable to. The sorrow had momentarily taken the front seat.

My feelings of having this time with Father Quem and Mother Sarah had been dashed and I thought about returning home instead of continuing my journey up the mountain. Then I thought about next week—the road would be closed—I had better take this opportunity now as it will be a long winter.

I turned the key to start Sarah Jane Blue's engine and drove toward the gate that lead up to Panther Meadows. I had thought about driving even further up the mountain if the road was clear.

One side of the road hugs the mountain and often there will be rocks that have fallen in the path of the cars. On the other side of the road, in places, there are steep drop-offs going down the mountain. Drivers and passengers alike are well aware of the hazards of this road.

Close to Panther Meadows, on the road, I began to see patches of black ice here and there. My anxiety level shot up several notches. Directly after the meadows, the road turned to a solid layer of ice.

It wasn't a nice smooth layer. From the looks of it, yesterday the road had been covered with a thick layer of slush that had frozen over-night producing a rough layer of ice with deep channels embedded where the cars and trucks had driven. I had driven about a quarter of a mile when I realized that this ice was not going to go away and decided I had to turn around.

Ironically, Nathanal had guided me to purchase my car, Sarah Jane, specifically for this type of terrain, yet… Quickly, I studied the width of the road and the steep drop over the side. Feelings of fear had erupted; I was scared to drive the car forward let alone turn it around! If I slipped, I risked either hitting the boulders, the trees or the mountain itself—I risked going over and down the precipice crashing through the trees, ending my descent God knows where. I tried to detach from my thoughts, my fear, and remain cool as I forced myself to shift the car into reverse and inch the car back a few feet. Then I shifted the car into drive going forward a few feet. I repeated my actions until I was completely turned around.

The sweat had begun to gather on my brow and between my breasts; so I opened the window for relief, all the while noting that the temperature gauge read 28 degrees.

I had managed to get turned around only to realize the gravity of my situation. There staring me straight in the face, I saw the steep downhill grade and the thick ruts of ice. My thoughts slipped into images of a perpetual slide downhill, just like the scene before me. What I had thought and envisioned had quickly escalated into a panic. But I had no choice except to go forward, inching along until I passed the icy area. I was on auto-pilot mode that was entirely fear-based. Even after the danger had passed, I did not stop or even pause to enjoy the scenery until twenty minutes later when I had arrived safely at the bottom of the mountain.

Feeling a tremor of fear in my body, I realized that I was totally out of balance. Then I recognized how easily I had overlooked my reason for going up the mountain in the first place. I had wanted to connect with nature, the mountain, and the Lemurians. However, I had not enjoyed my time on the mountain at all. I had fled in fear.

* * *

That night I had a dream so intense that I remembered it with great clarity when I woke up. I feel dreams are important and may assist us in processing our thoughts or perhaps they may be prophetic messages. It is quite possible that we are connecting with our soul family through that state. For those reasons, I interpret my dreams the best I can when I remember them. If I have difficulty with the interpretation, I ask my guides for assistance.

The images of my dream were powerful, invoking intense emotions. I broke down the scenes and working to understand the symbolism.

The first scene: I was walking behind a couple who were obviously in love. As they walked down the path they were playfully trying to slide love letters in each other's back pockets.

Scene Two: The man was suddenly gone—nowhere in sight.

Scene Three: The wind was blowing so strongly I feared for my safety. In the distance, I saw a woman in a neighborhood. She stood in an open area between houses. The grass was a vivid green and rain came down hard. The wind was the strongest in the area where the woman stood. I thought the wind might lift up the houses. From a distance, I watched the woman as she beckoned for me to join her. She didn't seem to be afraid of the storm. Although, I *knew* she wasn't safe. I *knew* that I would be in more danger if I went to her. She continued to motion for me to come to her. I just watched her. I was standing in front of a house where I was somewhat protected.

Scene Four: I saw the woman's body lifted and go sailing through the air toward to the southeast. I felt no one would ever see her again.

Scene Five: I went inside the house and found a small room for protection (the way you would in case of a tornado).

Initially, I thought the dream had something to do with the fact that my parents had gone back home to Pleiades.

But later it became evident that the dream was about my trip up Mt. Shasta.

Scene One: The man represents masculine side or logical, thinking side of me; and the woman is the feminine, emotional and feeling side of me. On the way up the mountain I was balanced in harmony with my feminine and masculine side. I was happy and felt love and even excitement that I was on a mystical journey with my family.

Scene Two: The man disappeared—my logical thinking. When my parents got out the car I became unbalanced as I leaned toward lower emotions—feelings of sadness, grief and abandonment. My parents, whom I adored, had gone; and I didn't know when I would be with them again.

Scene Three: As I drove up the mountain, I saw the black ice. Knowing the danger, I became more unbalanced—leaning more to feelings of fear than to logical problem solving. When I encountered the ice-covered roads, fear completely took over. This was when my survival instinct came into play. I was afraid for my life. The woman in the dream was the part of me that was in danger. I was clearly torn at that point. I had wanted to go further up the mountain but saw how reckless it was to do so. I was not safe if I continued on. Fear outweighed every logical thought. In fact, I was no longer thinking logically. I was only feeling that I was in danger.

Scene Four: The woman who stood unprotected was removed from the scene. I didn't listen to her tempt me to continue my journey.

Scene Five: When I had gone into the small room I put myself in a safer place—going down the mountain.

I had been writing for quite a while when I finally heard Babaró say, "You have most of your dream understood but not all of it. May I continue?" I was a little surprised because I had thought that I had done a really good job interpreting the dream, but I told Babaró, if there is more I'll certainly listen."

"The dream," Babaró said, "Is multifaceted and a tool that is quite useful to look at concerning what you are thinking and how you feel overall—if you are balanced and where you want to be in life. The dream showed you that you had been balanced but during the course of the journey of the day you had become unbalanced. The dream is perfect to teach you about your feelings—how attached you are to your parents and how you truly feel about traveling on the mountain no matter the weather or road conditions.

"I'd like to take the opportunity to point out that, up until this day, each time you have had an opportunity to drive up the mountain you have physically recoiled. This is not just a subtle thought or feeling here. You have been quite aware of the anxiety you felt when we encouraged you travel this road. Driving in the mountains is a trigger for you. Being in the mountains is a trigger." I knew Babaró was correct but didn't see the correlation with the dream.

"It has a lot to do with the dream, Nakala. Bear with me while I unravel your truth. Even though you are very connected to the Lemurians—they are your soul family—getting close to them brings fear. Remember the little boat full of frightened, shivering women? Remember your oath as a High Priestess to comfort those in distress—no matter what the circumstance? You gave up your life upholding your oath during the sinking of the continent of Lemuria. Nakala, to travel up that mountain near Telos is a trigger for you. You carry deep within you fear of the unpredictability of nature—its volatile character. It would be wise of you to look at this close-up and come to terms with it."

Moments passed and I heard no other words. I was emotionally spent. I called out to Babaró, "How do I fix this?" His response came swiftly, "With affirmations, Miss. 'I am always safe.'" I took a deep breath and shook my head not believing I had this other thing that I was to resolve—to heal.

My emotions were overtaking me and my breathing became erratic. The sensible thing to do was take a break from writing, yet I continued on. "Babaró, I felt I was very aware of the areas that I am to concentrate on concerning my healing; and then suddenly, out of left field, here is another issue. Will this ever end? Will I ever be free of fear?"

I stopped typing and began to speak to Babaró. "One of the reasons I came here to California was to work with Adama. This doesn't make sense." Babaró channeled a breath through me calming me before he began his explanation. "Nakala, you are torn. Part of you wants to be with your soul family and the other part is afraid of losing your life…again.

You would rather not travel up the mountain—in the open where the winds can carry you away to never be seen or heard of again. That is enough for now, Nakala. I have something else to bring forth…something closer to your heart.

"I speak of your Nathanal. He has taken on a project, shall we say, so the two of you may join on a more intimate level. I will traverse back a bit before I go forward. You have stated that you would like a mate to assist you in the workings of your life—to have a companion, a lover, a help-mate. This however tears at you because Nathanal, your twin flame, stands beside you in all that you do. Nathanal is your husband, the person you love with all of your heart, and to take on another seems to be a direct action disregarding, even disrespecting your husband, and seems cruel—unfair even though you desire someone in the physical to share your life with."

I was shaking my head in disbelief with Babaró's choice of topics to write about in this book! Well, if Babaró insisted on talking about it, so be it!

"It is true that I would like someone in a physical body to share my life with. I want to be able to go to a restaurant or a movie with someone that I can carry on a conversation with in the open instead of telepathically. I want to be free to exchange ideas, concepts, and pleasantries with this person. Yet, I have Nathanal who I love dearly. I mean he is everything to me; yet he is not in a physical body. Is it wrong of me to want to sit across the table and have a conversation with a man I can see, touch, hear and smell—who I care for and love? In my mind, I have gone round and round with this desire. On one hand, I feel I am cheating on Nathanal if I settle down with another man, but in the same moment I feel that my life is not fulfilled. Why is this so hard?" I was embarrassed, ashamed and perplexed, and with anger in tow, I blurted out, "Why are we even discussing this in this book?"

"Nakala, notice the title of this book, *In the Light of Day.* I chose that title and I ask you to take note of what the title implies. It is time that people stop hiding the way they feel—to come out in the open and express themselves freely."

In my mind's eye, this time it was Babaró who was shaking his head. "Nakala, you are here to have a physical experience. Do you not realize that you have had countless lives married to someone besides Nathanal—as he acted as guide for you just as in this go-around (incarnation)? Believe me, this is no big deal. You feel this way like you are cheating on Nathanal by even thinking of having a mate. Quite simply, it is social programing.

"We have told you that you are to have another to love on the Earth plane, to comfort and to assist. Rest assured the steps are being made for this to occur.

"The project I mentioned earlier that Nathanal has taken on—he is working with the man of your dreams. (I rolled my eyes then.) He is practicing with the man as a walk-in. Nathanal is joining in consciousness and at times projecting his own thoughts. Nathanal is also projecting his own feelings for this man to experience. Usually the thoughts and feelings are very subtle and the subject will not detect, at first, that they are not his own. You know all about this, Nakala, as Samuel Paul, myself and Nathanal join with you. This assists you on staying on track—more focused on your path while learning to stay more positive. Sometimes what we do is undetectable while other times you are quite aware that what has entered your mind is not your thought."

Babaró paused as he began to project a thought in my mind to remind me of something. I was excited because I knew what he was doing. When I got the thought I said, "Oh, I got it! Sunday when I suddenly wanted to drive up the mountain that was someone else's thought! I wondered about that. It was out of character for me to all of a sudden want to take off like that, especially to go on the mountain."

He nodded his head, smiled and simply said, "Indeed."

"Nathanal is working as a walk-in for this other fellow. He is preparing all for the physical melding of energies between the two of you." I felt a little put off and asked, "Why don't you just tell me his name? Saying this man or this fellow...I don't like it."

"Nakala, I will not share this man's name with you because the experience is a gift to you—a surprise. Let it all play out and have fun!"

PART
FOUR

TO THINE OWN SELF
BE TRUE

CHAPTER
TWENTY-ONE

Babaró had given me the directive, "You are to take the day off from writing. Do something that you will enjoy."

I had found that it is wise not to fight his guidance especially when it comes to writing. Babaró will flat-out refuse to assist me.

After what Babaró had shared with me about what Nathanal was doing—where he had been going most of the days while I had been writing—the melding of energies with the man who remained nameless, I really needed to have some time to process my feelings. For me, writing is the easiest way to look at the total picture.

However, in this particular case I wasn't sure I had been given the entire picture! So I intentionally laid aside my thoughts concerning the matter.

It was all good, I reasoned, that I could seize the opportunity and use the day for creative purposes, work on a couple of art projects and then later, maybe do a little house cleaning.

The feelings of being unsettled persisted, though, as I thought about all the shifts taking place in my life—and in my guidance. Sakeem would be working with this new *fellow* part of the time; then Nathanal would go while I wrote with Babaró. It was if the two of them, Sakeem and Nathanal, were playing tag-team with this guy. Jonson was making himself more available and assured me that he would be around to assist me more. (Jonson is the guide with the Texas drawl stationed in Telos.)

In addition, a new guide who is an artist, Rebeka had shown up a couple of weeks ago. It had been revealed that she would channel artwork through me.

On several occasions, I had asked if I could please get a new guide to channel the portraits for me. I had wanted to, at least, get Babaró's portrait.

Several years ago, Tirclé (a female artist/guide) channeled through me several portraits of the beings I work with. Since then, Tirclé had reincarnated and was no longer available to work with me.

Finally, Rebeka had shown up answering my request...or so I had thought.

I had been so excited to have her that I had asked to work with her at a particular segment that really wasn't free. That day I just hadn't had the time or the energy to sit and draw although, for some reason, I wouldn't set the idea aside and wait until I was more relaxed. I had *wanted* a picture of Babaró!

So on a week-day evening, in between writing and cooking dinner, I had hastily gathered together my pencils and sketch tablet and sat down on my emerald-green recliner to draw.

It had been well established that Rebeka and I would join on *Sundays* to draw portraits and possibly do some watercolors, as well. Even so, since she was there, I called for her and then waited for her to speak.

Well, the session with Rebeka had turned out to be a total disaster. During our time together, I had not been able to relax and allow her to work through me. I was not relaxed at all. At some point, I wanted to try again.

Rebeka explained that I was not acclimated to her energy, so she had told me that she would spend time with me for that to take place. For some reason something didn't jive. However, I accepted her explanation. What else could I do?

All in all, I knew that I had been adjusting to the new guidance/energy. I questioned if, on some level, I might be resisting these changes.

On several occasion, my guides had deliberately mixed things up: my schedule, who I channeled and so on. I suspected that this might be one of those times. If so, I was being given the same lesson again: To detach from my regular schedule, my guides—my perception of life, in general.

Of course, I knew that being attached would cause me to stumble and ultimately fall. Being attached will bring about lower emotions and might impede growth. My guides brought me comfort. I depended on my guides and not to be somewhat attached was, well, maybe asking a little much at the moment.

I wanted confirmation with my overview so I asked, "Babaró, I think I may have become a little too attached to my way of doing things. Is that why my schedule and my guides are changing? I mean for the most part, except for Nathanal, there isn't a one of you (the guides) that are going to allow me to become attached to your guidance."

"Nakala, dearest, you know that your father, Quem has appointed me as guardian for you. As guardian—master teacher, I watch over you very closely and one of your life lessons is the lesson of detachment. To be attached to any person or thing may prove to be unhealthy and may slow you down or even prevent you from fulfilling your sacred contract. With our guidance you will deal with the issue and certainly overcome.

"The energy of attachment is confining and a denser energy that holds back not only you, but will hold others back, as well. People are to follow their own sacred journey freely.

"When Quem and Sarah got out of the car Sunday (the trip to Mt. Shasta) to go on their walk you felt a sense of sadness because they are your parents and to have them around had been pleasing. You felt like you had a real family even though the rest of us are with you always: Samuel Paul, Stephanó, Nathanal and I.

We have been constant with your care. We are your family. Your feelings stem from not having your biological parents nearby and involved in your daily life. This is an inner child issue and one that is nearly healed. You have shifted from your neediness concerning your biological parents to a minor longing to have them near and the desire to keep them safe as they age."

⁕ ⁕ ⁕

"Nakala, the weather here has shifted again. You have blue skies and the temperature is pleasing. You seem to have ants in your pants as you are distracted with thoughts of taking yourself outdoors to work in the yard—to breathe the fresh air—be in nature. I ask you to please focus on the task at hand for a short while longer."

Babaró was correct. I wanted out of my office and outdoors and answered, "All I can say right now is I'll do my best."

Babaró stopped speaking to me and I stopped writing because I saw the paradox—the irony of it all. One of the very first teachings I had received was to follow my heart—do what makes my heart sing. Usually, writing is what I want to do. However, right now to sit here at my desk and write felt like I was being held against my will. I was not happy. I wanted to be outdoors. Yet not to work on my writing I believed to be very irresponsible. My guides had specifically told me that we would work certain days. (What I do is just like a job. I get ready for work, arrive on time, and on the designated days.) Not to follow through seemed very wrong. There was a line here: Do I go outside because I want to or do I write because I should?

"Exactly!" said Babaró. "There are segments, cycles or seasons for everything. Today is a beautiful day and because it has been nearly ten days since you were last outdoors tending to your place, you feel very drawn to go. Honor yourself and go. The pages will wait."

* * *

I went out and raked up the pine needles. They had gotten hung up in the bushes and flowers like Christmas ornaments, so I sat down on the earth and lost myself in the activity of picking them off. To get down there with the plants felt refreshing! I breathed in the scents of lavender, thyme, other plants, and even the soil.

After a couple of hours at it, Babaró said, "Nakala, it is time to get back to writing. You have cleared the energy that caused you to feel restless. Getting some physical exercise is part of balancing. Sometimes you require getting up to stretch or just walking out the door to get some fresh air. To deny yourself is to purposefully add to your imbalance."

* * *

"Nakala," Babaró continued, "You are learning some valuable lessons. We are pleased with your progress. However, it continues to come down to the very same thing: Listen to your heart and follow it."

> *This above all: To thine own self be true,*
> *And it must follow, as the night the day,*
> *Thou canst not then be false to any man.*
> ~Shakespeare-*Hamlet*

Even though, I had come to this place of understanding—this revelation, I said, "I am not entirely satisfied, Babaró." I made a commitment to write the books—to act as the designated scribe for you; and to turn my back on that, well…it is like having a paying job. I clock-in at a certain time and I clock-out when my day is finished. It doesn't matter if I don't *feel* like working or not.

Babaró shook his head and sighed. In his voice I thought I heard a tinge of sadness as he said, "That is the old paradigm. When you move into the fifth dimensional energy, everything changes. You join with your Higher Self on a conscious level, going forward, and when all comes into alignment to do something you do it! You work with us! We will never request you to work when you are feeling from your heart a greater pull to do something else. Never!" Finally, I saw all the pieces and replied, "Yes, I see it finally. I understand. Thank you, Babaró."

"Honey," Babaró added, "Know that you are being tested always. Your structure must be strong—flexible but unbreakable."

Babaró moved on with his teaching. "On another note, concerning your writing, you require breaks—many. The physical body was created to move about not to sit for lengthy periods of time in front of a computer screen. To sit causes the circulatory system to slow down, inviting stagnation and toxins to take residence. To be healthy and continue the flow of energy, you are to move the body to stimulate. We desire you not to create a body that is stiff and flabby that encourages blocks of denser energy to hang about. In other words, we desire the physical body to be healthy and feel good—balanced! How you treat the body affects all that you are and do, Nakala."

CHAPTER
TWENTY-TWO

"Seriously another trip?" was all I could muster. I had only been in California a little over two months and now I was being guided to go to Turkey. For me this was beyond the call of duty. Because I had an attitude, I had been instructed to practice this affirmation on a daily basis: *Throughout all situations, I am in alignment with what my Higher Self guides me to do on all levels of consciousness.*

To be on the road so much could be exhilarating but there were times that it was best to rest. Sometimes, I just wanted to take it easy and be in one place and not be forced to be on a strict regimen. The trip was set to take place the next April. Perhaps by then I would be ready to go.

However, at the moment I was having a little issue with the decision. I had seen pictures of Istanbul and it was quite a beautiful place. Still, I had no desire to go. What I felt was completely different than what I felt when I was called to move to California. Turkey? My heart was not in it.

My guides said that I was to go for several reasons. One, I required material for the books. Two, there were activations that were to be made by the group that had contracted to go. Three, I was to go for the experience. I am a Pleiadian Traveler and I was in training to take over, with Nathanal, the responsibility of leading the Kingdom of Myra. Any and all experiences would assist in this endeavor.

So why was I having such a difficult time with this?

"I will speak on this Nakala," Babaró declared. "First off, you have free will. If you do not wish to go, then don't. But I know, as well as your other guides do, that it is your Mother's and Father's desire that you do go.

"There are several reasons that you resist this trip. Shall we go over them?" As I inhaled deeply, I realized how tired I was concerning this subject. If I heard the word Turkey again…well, I just would rather move on.

Something in particular was bothering me—my first teaching, which was to listen to my heart concerning all matters. "Babaró," I began I do not and have not felt the desire in my heart to go to Turkey—not once. I feel to go would not be honoring myself. However, I see the wisdom in going. I also wonder if sometimes Mother Sarah and Father Quem would much rather stay at home instead of traveling all over. Do they go because it is for the higher good? But if they are weary from the travel how can it be for the higher good?"

"Nakala, these are all great insights and good questions that you have presented. My response is, as a leader in training to learn discernment is of great import. Because you are residing in a physical body you must discern what is for the greater good of it! Intuitively, you know that you require rest.

"In the last few years, we requested that you take several international trips—you did. In addition, you physically moved your personal household four times. This has all taken place in the last—how many years?" He paused for a while waiting for me to answer him. "Babaró, it is all a blur. Honestly, I don't know when this began."

"I will tell you, Nakala," Babaró stated. "The first trip to Italy was three years ago. All four moves took place in the last two and a half years. In addition to that, you cleaned out your father's estate and sold his home. There were many other legal issues that were taken care of during this time."

At this time, I stopped writing, pushed my keyboard back and began looking through my calendars, checkbooks and files to find the dates that all of these moves and legal procedures supposedly took place. It isn't that I didn't believe Babaró; it was that I didn't think what I had done was possible!

As I began to make notes on when I had traveled and moved, I was astounded by how swift each major change had come about. Babaró was correct on when the moves began and how *many* changes had occurred!

I was just plain tired. Logically, I reasoned this is the reason that, now, I just wanted to rest.

I saw the similarity in the situations of writing and going outside with staying home and taking yet another international trip. I wanted to go outside and I wanted to stay at home—I needed time to breathe and balance! The only difference I could see was the trip to Turkey was scheduled in the future. I would have time to rest beforehand.

Babaró suddenly stopped me. He channeled the motion of me pressing my hand to my heart as he said in an authoritative voice, "Listen to your heart, Nakala."

All I could say was, "I do not want to let my parents down." Suddenly, with the utmost clarity, I saw the lesson over and over again being presented to me in different scenarios—to thine own heart be true. I laughed and shook my head. "Wow, this is the big one, isn't it, Babaró?"

As he nodded his head, I heard him breathe deeply and say in agreement, "Oh, yes."

A giant weight had been lifted that I had carried for three months. But I still wondered if my decision not to go to Turkey stemmed from fear. I was sure there were so many benefits to going on the trip. But no matter how good the trip sounded, I still felt I needed to rest. I simply wanted to stay home and *be* here.

CHAPTER
TWENTY-THREE

For two days I didn't write a single word. Instead I played with my art projects.

The previous week Babaró had suggested that I add a character directory in the books—specifically, *The Sacred Contract,* which is currently being edited. His suggestion had triggered a memory. I dug out different journals that I had made notes in concerning the different guides that had come and given me messages. I realized that pronunciation of the guides' name, for me even, had been a huge issue. Undoubtedly, for the reader, it would be important to be able to pronounce the names correctly, so it was decided that we should add the phonetics to each name. But what other information would be beneficial for the reader to have? I began to compile everything I knew about each character who had appeared in the book. As I completed my research, I saw Babaró's name had precious little after it.

As my master guide—my guardian—what exactly did I know about him? From the looks of my compilation, I did not know a whole heck of a lot. For at least the last two years I had consistently asked for an artist to channel through me a portrait of him and received zilch—nada…

Early on I learned that if the guides didn't want to talk about themselves, they won't. In conclusion, I stopped asking any of my guides personal questions. Obviously, they felt teaching me God's Laws were way more important. I had to agree with them on that.

However, when I looked at Babaró's entry in the directory and saw that I didn't even have a middle name for him, I began to formulate my questions. I asked, "Babaró did you tell me your middle name? Babaró what do you look like anyway?"

Babaró didn't speak, but in my mind's eye I saw a heavier man with longish hair and full beard. I wasn't getting that he was particularly tall or handsome either. Just who was this man other than Quem's brother and my guardian?

Babaró remained silent, so I let it go.

During the following night, I had a weird dream but it wasn't exactly a dream. I had been in a semi-conscious state. I had received a name during this time: Henry Wadsworth Longfellow. The name came at me over and over. One time, I heard the name James Wadsworth Longfellow. In my sleep state I said to myself, "No, that isn't correct." Then I heard the time period had been the eighteen hundreds.

When I woke up the name jumped at me again. *Why did I get that name?* Then Babaró did something that I would never have imagined in a hundred years. He announced that he had been this man—lived that life.

I pondered the name and vaguely remembered that this man was someone famous. Henry Wadsworth Longfellow might have been a poet or a writer. I just wasn't sure. I didn't waste any time. I went straight to the computer and did a search on him. For those of you who do not know of this man, he had been a famous poet/writer/teacher and he lived in the eighteen hundreds. Babaró...Henry Wadsworth Longfellow.

Henry Wadsworth Longfellow
1807-1882

Babaró is in the writing business; I knew that. He told me that he is not now married (or in a relationship). He is in service to expedite his evolution—therefore man's evolution.

I still find it uncanny that Babaró would wait all of these years before he decided to reveal something this substantial to me!

In retrospect, though, I can clearly see Babaró's handiwork—his finesse. Candidly, he instructed me to create a directory. In complying with his request I saw the lack of information concerning him—I saw how little I actually knew about him. Perhaps if he had disclosed this information sooner I might have been intimidated to work with him? Whatever his reason, his admission had a keen impact on me.

* * *

Sensing Babaró's desire to speak, I stopped my writing and cleared my mind, waiting to hear him begin his message. "Yes, I desire to have my say. I waited. Yes, I waited to tell you because simply it was a past life and an experience at that. I am not that person. Instead, I look at it as that was my expression—an experience. I am a summation of all of my lives and my experiences.

"Having accrued a vast vocabulary and ability to write in many fascinating styles, I consider myself to be a veteran of literary structures. In addition, I am no longer held down nor bound by the desires of the flesh. This does not mean I am not a feeling man, because I am! The beauty that I see and feel is beyond any written prose that I may batter out. To touch a scrap of royal blue velvet fabric stirs my senses. For the love of it all—God's creation in His vast expanse."

It was here that I became confused. Babaró used the terminology of senses. I have physical senses because I am in a physical body. "What senses are you referring to Babaró?" I asked.

"Ah"…Babaró sighed. Then he replied, "The senses of the mind! Everything is experienced through the mind. I can look upon a beautiful woman and be drawn in by God's magnificence—His creation. This is what stirs—God's creation. Nakala, I wish you to lay down the pen and paper for today. Allow yourself to rest with the information that you have gleaned thus far. We will reconvene again tomorrow morning."

* * *

"As the new dawn breaks through so does the silence, the stillness, of God." Those were the first words uttered by Babaró this morning. The receiving of his words drew forth a profound measure of emotion—tears.

Babaró seemed to be free now to express himself more to his liking as his style of dictation changed. "I, thus far, have been careful of my dictation—not speaking in a manner that perhaps offends or even delights on an absurd level. The writings of the nineteenth century were quite obtrusive in comparison to what is being contributed in today's literary world.

"In addition, we are teaching you God's Truths and our emphasis has not been on exposing the wafts of seductive perfumes or the writhing of blood and gore that is predominant in some descriptive writing. Although, for you, perhaps this is what drives you: to be a temptress, beguiling and alluring in the way you are able to stir, with words alone, the physical senses and emotion of the mind and heart."

"Oh, Babaró," I said, "you have me pegged alright. To evoke the senses of the reader in such a way that they *feel* they are one with the story—they feel they are literally in the story—has been my objective, my challenge. I have struggled with this because the books I currently write to me seem severe. Somehow, I want to incorporate more description and feeling into the text. However, I have not been guided to do this. When I ask the reason for this, I am simply told these are not the kinds of books for that. I am sorry but I want to carry the reader away, far away into a land that is thought provoking, stirring the senses and emotions, bringing them to a place of total healing and wellness. I know what I want to achieve…it is just getting there."

Babaró had stood back watching me write, listening to me formulate my thoughts into words—changing them until I was satisfied. But above all as he stood beside me, he was feeling my love that I have for the written word.

"Nakala, you wonder why I, a master, who is held in high esteem, would desire to work with you and the Comterous instead of seeking out another incarnation on Earth, thus allowing me to possibly become an ascended master alongside my brothers, Stephanó and Samuel Paul? My choice stems from light and darkness. It is because in this realm there is no decay or death. I am not caught-up in the endless void of the unknown like I was when I held a physical body.

"My incarnation as Henry Wadsworth Longfellow brought forth much esteem, much grandeur. But through the untimely losses of life and my undeniable perception that I could not go forward without certain influences and love from another on the realm of the physical, I dipped heavily into the man-made reality of absolute, unforgettable misery. For me to step, both knowingly and unknowingly, into a miasma of gigantic proportions again is to risk my delicate nature to the open hands of the gentle soul bound to be forever tortured in the fiery pits of hell itself. I think it best I serve in this way for now."

I was stunned by Babaró's intimate revelation; and for the moment, I didn't how to respond. Instead, of trying to plod through my thoughts, I asked for a break from writing. I felt emotionally drained by Babaró's words and possibly his choices. At any rate, I got up and headed for the kitchen. But as I stood up an odd sensation made itself known in my mind—my body. Call it a knowing or possibly a keen sense of distrust that I may have been played or duped. Then I heard Babaró say, "That is why I am called the master."

I furrowed my eyebrows and deliberately walked past him saying, "You are good, really good." It was at that moment I knew Babaró had a grand scheme—a master plan. To see how he played his next hand was sure going to be interesting. For now, I just had a headache that was getting bigger.

I took an hour lunch and still didn't feel like returning to my office. I said out loud, "Maybe I'll take a sick day." With that Babaró rapidly shot back that left no room for conjecture, "No, you will not. You are not sick." Then he said, "It is time to come back to it."

"Okay, I am back. I am sitting at my computer and I feel that I must voice my disbelief. Babaró, I feel it quite possible you made up this Longfellow story."

I went on laying out the steps that Babaró had so brilliantly set before me. "Last night, you had me download Longfellow's biography from Wikipedia, disclosing his delicate nature and long suffering not only from the death of two of his children and his two wives, but also from a certain intolerance or perhaps jealousy in some of his peers in the literary field of poetry. Longfellow had grieved plenty (never recovering fully), especially after his second wife had died from burns. He worried he would go insane and begged "not to be sent to an asylum" and noted that he was "inwardly bleeding to death". But he had also led an affluent life, studying abroad, learning several languages, being the highest paid poet of that era. Longfellow was a professor first at Bowdoin College and then at Harvard. Longfellow was also well-known for his detailed ability to translate foreign prose. One of his greatest accomplishments was his translation of Dante Alighieri's *Divine comedy*, which took him several years to complete. His problem did not stem from financial deprivation but from emotional depression.

Quite simply, I didn't know what to make of what I had been told or led to believe. Suddenly, Babaró began channeling several deep breaths through me until I felt a little light-headed. Then I waited for Babaró to begin his teaching, which I knew, this time, was going to be a real doozy.

"I certainly did not mislead you. Longfellow or I played the part well to express human suffering and also human success, do you not think so?"

"Well," I began, "He—you made many significant contributions to the human race, especially in education within the affluent community. It stands to reason that no one can have it all. Perhaps his life—your life— was kept more in balance with the successes and the suffering. It seems, though, the highs and lows were excessive. I really don't know."

Babaró sighed as if contemplating my take on *his* "story" and that is really all it was—a story.

"Yes, it is a story," Babaró said, "a made-up performance by yours truly. And I dare say quite spectacular in the way that I (with the assistance of many others), experienced, or should I say, created a reality that was fantastical. It seems it could have come straight from someone's imagi- nation—a fairy tale, perhaps. The thing is it did—from my and the other player's imaginations, that is!

"What I would like to bring to the forefront that is quite compelling: a sizeable portion of that life was created because I was not aware of what I was doing on all counts—just like most of the people on Earth do not understand in fullness the true and undeniable fact that they are creating their reality with thoughts, emotions and actions. A great deal of the time your thoughts are so out of control you have no idea what you are creating or where your drive originates let alone what your spiritual purpose is.

"I am your master teacher and at this time I am focused on your ascension—your steps forward. In order to go forward as the God-Being that you truly are you must be in full control—cognizant of what you are thinking and feeling in every moment. So my life—my happiness as well as my sorrows as Henry Wadsworth Longfellow has been well worth it because I am using that life as a fine example for not only you but for countless others to set your priorities and hold fast to them. In other words— I was obsessive with my studious nature—making a mark on the world. I took the words, melding them into positions as to cause the reader to swoon and at times taking them into great heights as well as great lows. That was my ambition.

"Nakala, you were told that the first book you published, *When Angels Speak*, did its work by just being written. As you wrote the words, immeasurable torrents of emotion flooded the etheric realm transforming great waves of negativity into Light!

"Books and other types of media are powerful tools to transform energy. It is best not to take anything for granted.

"By writing *When Angels Speak*, you were able to pay back almost every thread of karma that you had created in the summation of your past lives and what you had created in this life as well. You are nearly finished with that aspect of clearing. We are pleased."

CHAPTER
TWENTY-FOUR

From what I could discern, Babaró was a passionate and gentle soul who had taken the embodiment of Henry Wadsworth Longfellow. Longfellow had been highly motivated in the literary field stating plainly, "I will not disguise it in the least…the fact is, I most eagerly aspire after future eminence in literature, my whole soul burns most ardently after it, and every earthy thought centres in it…I am almost confident in believing, that if I can ever rise in the world it must be by the exercise of my talents in the wide field of literature."

I could see that his attention had been fixed, seeing himself at the top of *the* hill working to perfect his skills and making a nice living at it, to add to the mix. However, I almost saw his writing as an obsession of sorts.

Babaró cut me off then saying, "That is what I did—my writing—my livelihood…my passion! This was—is one way of expressing myself."

Suddenly, I felt a shift and heard Babaró say, "Ah, I get on with it. This writing is my heart's passion. It was then and it is now! You think I was/ am obsessed perhaps because I am constantly looking for a way to convey the messages that will be forthright bearing God's Truth?

"In my life as Longfellow, I wrote stories in the form of poetry. This was what the readers were hungry for at the time. My descriptive writing was lyrically and strategically woven in the stanzas, awakening further the readers through elegance and rhythm."

I continued to be somewhat puzzled by Longfellow's elegant life coupled with severe depression. So I asked, "Babaró am I incorrect in my summation? Through your writings, your ideals, it was like you were writing a script of sorts attaching great surges of emotion to them—the poems reflected your state of mind. On a lower level of consciousness weren't you ignorant of this alchemy?...The way I see it, the more you wrote, the more emotion poured through and out of you into the ethers. You were literally caught in a processional maelstrom—living it and writing it, then writing it and living it. Through your writings you were precariously caught up in the magnetic tides of thought, emotion and action. When any event, be it tragic or a happy one, you faithfully, artistically and emotionally expressed yourself through your writing to have it only gain more momentum to the point of taking you either high up on the mountain in a state of delirious achievement or down into a deep gully of despair."

"What I have set before you," Babaró began, "is a teaching of extremes. Yet, I ask you, is it all that extreme—my life as Longfellow, in comparison to the people of today, or of any day on the sweet Earth, for that matter? Longfellow's life—my life—quietly mimicked their lives, the drama, their belief that they are the story. I put it in the past tense but this is incorrect. My life as Longfellow mimics their lives, their drama, still to this day as my stories are still read and reread and given flight to the ethers.

"Kings and queens of drama—this is what the human species have taken themselves to be instead of the glorious God-Beings they truly are. The human species have inhabited the Earth for eons. It has come— this is the apex in your evolution to take stock of what you think, feel and do in all moments of your life. I say again, it has come; this is the apex for you to access and assess your innermost secrets, your thoughts, knowing fully the repercussions of where your focus lies. You are to rise above the drama of bigotry, scandal, lust, hate and *fear—the lower energies of man.*

"I have given you a prime example for grand success as my life as Longfellow. I was more successful than any other poet of that era. Yet, I managed to sink in the muck and mire of my own unintentional making."

Babaró continued on. "I can give you more teachings on the Law of Attraction if you like; but the matter of it is—no matter the examples or stories I recount, you must do the work—you must be in control of your mind.

"I give you this Nakala, I loved my wife—I adored her. She was the undeniable reason for my living. When the most hideous of tragedies struck and she was swiftly and unjustly taken from me in front of my very eyes in the most dreadful of ways, how could I not take it deep into my bosom? I literally burned for her immediate and complete resurrection and her unwavering companionship." (Babaró was working to explain Longfellow's years of depression, his inability to write.)

At that moment, I decided to take a long break from writing, as was my habit. Upon returning, I reread the last sentence—Babaró's declaration concerning his wife. I gasped with the realization of his depth of despair and how he had put it into words with a double meaning. "I literally burned for her immediate and complete resurrection and her unwavering companionship." This was his summation of his last act for his wife, Francis Elizabeth. (Francis's dress caught on fire. Longfellow had been napping and woke up. He tried to put it out with a small throw rug and in doing so he had suffered severe burns himself—bad enough to not be able to attend her funeral. Francis died the next day.

CHAPTER
TWENTY-FIVE

Today is the sixth of November, an unseasonal but comfortable 63 degrees. I had been living in California almost three months. Not one day had I grieved for my old life in Kansas. Some days I thought of my family and wished I could be with them, but those thoughts and feelings were fleeting—I did not set my focus on them.

All morning, Stephanó has waited patiently for his time to write with me—until Babaró had been finished with what he wanted to contribute to this book.

As I sat at my computer, I began on a conscious level to breath rhythmically before I said, "Thank you Stephanó for your gifts—for what I am about to receive."

Stephanó said, "Often, you wonder about your guides—us—our lives beyond our service to humanity and that includes our personal service to you. Nakala, I have always kept my personal life to myself when it comes to you. Yes, I do have a personal life; we all do. There are disciplines, rituals and other activities that we partake in to stay balanced.

"First, I'd like to speak on what we encounter when we work with the people who are currently of a lower vibration in the physical bodies, who have a lower awareness, hence a lower vibration. When we come into a person's field, such as this, we are subjected to a lesser degree or slower vibration. Consequently, we are susceptible to falling into the dense energy ourselves. We must be vigilant, as you must be as well, of the mechanics of our beings. Like a precise instrument, perhaps like an engine, we are liable to the accumulation of the everyday dirt and grime. We must be cleansed daily in order to maintain our rhythm and perfection. We go to our place of choice—be it temples, nature, or perhaps even another star or planet to meld with the sacred flames to purify, transmute and energize. This is on an inner level.

"In the etheric realm, there are strings of beautiful temples that represent the God-given attributes or gifts that we exemplify. Often, we visit these places to bring higher our vibration and expand our consciousness. We, too, seek higher states of transcendence.

"Just as you do, to remain in a balanced state, we must discipline ourselves and bring higher our vibration, never wavering from our love to serve God.

"On a more personal note, as I have stated before, I am an ascended master, doctor surgeon and your father, Quem's brother. There are a variety of councils I attend; with some I hold membership; in others I am in leadership. These councils are on the cutting-edge in a variety of areas—the sciences, the medical field, astrology, physics, the arts, communications, technology and education to name a few. Tirelessly, we offer your communities information that assists with evolution. Constantly there is an influx of new ideas coming to the minds of those who receive. I come as a benevolent Being of Light to serve humanity for the highest benefit.

"I laugh, Nakala, without question, you invariably gravitate toward questions concerning our family life. Nevertheless, we are witnessing a major shift: you are becoming more interested in the methodology of controlling energy.

"I'll answer your question as to whether I have a mate—a female companion or counterpart. I say, I am not focused on this type of a relationship (in the manner to which you refer) at this time. I have a twin flame who is embodied. I am detached with the goings on connected with the physicality of her expression. However, I continue to assist this one. One day, we will join again…As for now, my focus is on what makes my heart sing—my union with the ever present One, I AM, my service, my family, my friendships and my studies. I do bring in the joy in all aspects of my life. I am not stuffy like some would believe—you. There is always cause for celebration!"

✳ ✳ ✳

Stephanó's dictation stopped and he announced, "I must take leave." I thanked him for his message and opened my mind to remember who else wanted to work on the book today—who was it that had talked to me early this morning stating that he had words for me? Then the name, Sakeem came to me. I smiled as I recounted his words…I will assist you on your blog. These guys are incredible. Some days I wonder how I may ever repay them for all that they do. They remind me that they are assisting us because they love us, not because they desire or require something in return.

I felt Sakeem's presence to my right as he stood beside me. It looked like he was reading the words that I typed but perhaps he was patiently waiting for me to be quiet.

Then my attention was suddenly drawn outdoors to the croaking of a tree frog. Was he looking for a mate? For some reason I felt concerned that he should find himself a place to winter-over.

Then I heard, "Nakala, dearest, it is time." I knew Sakeem was ready to channel his message. He gave a simple nod and channeled a single deep breath through me reminding me to relax. "This time," he said, "the words are to be communicated differently." As he made his statement I understood his meaning. I didn't hear the words like usual, but knew what he was saying—what he wanted me to type. "Nakala, the process is simple: relax and enjoy."

I hadn't realized that I was tense, but then I noticed beads of perspiration had gathered on my neck, forehead and the middle of my back. Then I felt Sakeem's energy and my vibration began to rise. I wiped the wetness off of my forehead and wondered why all of the sudden I didn't feel so great. I took a sip of Jasmine tea and felt the warmth flow down into my body and spread outward as if it were alive and this was its sole purpose.

The memory came to the surface of my mind of last night's adventure. Someone had prompted me to rise from my seat and walk outdoors. The realization that the moon was full had suddenly came to mind. Whoever it had been, they had wanted to please me as I was being been drawn— guided to walk outdoors to partake in its beauty, its energy. With so many tall trees, it was difficult to see the sky let alone the moon. The alignment of the moon had to be just so for it to be in my sight.

As I walked outdoors and down the steep terrace off my patio, I was filled with anticipation of sorts—not really knowing what I'd see. I had felt like a child once again, full of wonder.

As I stepped around the corner I gasped at the site before me. Clouds had surrounded the moon and were moving past it in a mystical way. It was truly a beautiful sight.

Sakeem then repeated his words, "I am going to project the information to you a little differently today. The topic that we are to discuss is walk-ins and braid-ins." He had immediately engaged my interest as I had for some time waited for one of the guides to teach on this exact subject.

First, Sakeem stated, "Little mention is made of this phenomenon even in the metaphysical field. Yet it is a common occurrence. My aim today is to widen the scope of understanding in this area."

"To begin with, I will explain what a walk-in is. As a spiritual being you are a complex divine matrix of energy having many levels of conscious and different levels of attainment—states of being. You also have numerous energetic bodies and chakras or energy centers or points. You, as a collective, are just beginning to understand the divine cosmic matrix—how you are constructed. My aim is not to confuse you by defining all of your parts and their professions, but to explain that as a spiritual being you are a walk-in yourself. You, as a spiritual being, have walked-in to the physical body and are communicating and creating through it.

"Our topic isn't really about the fact that you walked in to a physical body. However, I wanted to emphasize—clarify that that is what you all have done. You are simply using the flesh body as an avenue for God's expression and to evolve.

"The term 'walk-in' that this teaching outlines is when another joins you in sharing the physical vehicle. Recently, you have been privy to the knowledge that Samuel Paul who is an ascended master has walked into the body you currently inhabit—he is currently sharing it with you.

"I'd like to go back in time, as you know it. When you were gifted with clairvoyance, clairaudience and the like, you were being attuned and activated to another level of consciousness that was braiding in to your lower consciousness: this is classified as a braid-in. Your name was changed from Jackie Mullinax to Nakala Akasie to reflect that shift in consciousness.

"Nakala, you have heard the term braid-in. It is similar to what a walk-in is. However, it is a different process. A braid-in is the process of the higher or expanded level of consciousness flowing into the crown—lower mind. (Sakeem projected to me an image of a spiral coming downward and entering my head.) In essence, your crown has opened somewhat allowing the flow of energy from the higher mind to come through you and join or braid-in with your own thoughts. You are receiving communications or information from a higher source to be filtered or braided into the lower mind to be expressed through the physical body. The braid-in is completed over a period of time—months or even years or even lifetimes before it is all-inclusive. The activations that you receive are to assist in this development.

"Now, to get back to the walk-ins. Samuel Paul came to you one day and stated, 'Nakala, I am to join with you.'" "Yes, I remember, Sakeem. What he said to me wasn't clear. I didn't understand his meaning although I didn't ask him to clarify his statement.

"On a conscious level, from that day on, Samuel Paul really stopped speaking to me. I have not received any teachings from him either. The only thing that I found different was when I asked, 'Samuel Paul, where are you?' Instantly, he would move my hands to my heart. Over the months, I would ask Samuel Paul the same question receiving the same channeled movement.

"Then there were times when my attention would be directed to something in particular or I would suddenly want to do something for no apparent reason or my body would be taken over completely like when I was in a store and suddenly I would be taken to another isle and shown something specific. But I am used to that. I mean there are times when I drive my car when all of a sudden someone else is driving through me. Sometimes I am okay with it, other times it scares me as it comes on so suddenly."

"Yes, Nakala these are some of the quirky things that you experience as a channel. As an ascended master, Samuel Paul has much experience at sitting back and overseeing. He is objective to a fault. Samuel Paul assesses all of your thoughts, feelings and actions, inserting or adding to or even shifting on a minor scale or more expanded scale at his own discretion, if you will, establishing more balance in your steps forward."

At that point my vibration escalated and I asked, "Samuel Paul is that you?" Samuel Paul then channeled a nod, a yes, but no words were spoken. I groaned. "Sakeem, this is all so weird!"

Sakeem continued his teaching to clarify. "Not really. Just consider your body having two energies running it—like a twin engine. You are the primary engine and the second engine only kicks in for assistance. His work is on a subtle level often going undetected."

Just then I got up to get some fresh tea. While I was in the kitchen, I thought about more on the subject of walk-ins and braid-ins being a "common occurrence". I wanted him to expand on his statement but waited to ask until I had returned to my computer so I could accurately record his response.

I was getting the sense that there were many of us with these so called walk-ins and braid-ins. When I returned to my office and got settled I asked, "Sakeem, are there people walking around in today's society that have walk-in or braid-ins and don't know it?"

"Oh, yes, many! It is one of the various ways for us to assist humanity." Mystified, I shook my head as if to clear it. I needed a more expanded explanation. "Wait a minute here," I said. "What happened to the rule of asking, allowing and accepting divine guidance?"

"Nakala, I'll be happy to answer all of your questions. The walk-ins and braid-ins generally occur on a sub-conscious level. When you ask, allow and accept, this is a practice that is incorporated on a conscious level. At that point you are creating an intention to work with the masters, angels, guides and your Higher Self on a conscious level. That is a step up and signifies that you are taking responsibility for your spiritual path."

Then I went on to ask, "Well, how come the subject hasn't been talked about that much?" But Sakeem shifted the subject before he answered my question.

"I have a gift for you just now, Nakala." I hesitated to type his words, but Sakeem nodded toward the computer screen simply saying, "Put it."

"Nakala, I feel your energy and it wanes a bit. You have other things to do tonight. However, first I have one last thing to share with you before I stop the transmission. You are being gifted. Know it. Samuel Paul has taken on an assignment that many would find tedious. However, because of his focus he is able to continue forth in a steadfast manner. He has taken on a role like a mother of one who is about ready to leave the nest—just watching and waiting in case there is a time when he is needed. Perhaps I'll give this example here. Your own children are grown and yet you stand back just on the edge (they know you are available) in case you are needed or wanted for advice. Concerning their lifestyles you say nothing, unless you are invited to do so."

I wanted to know more about this "relationship" with Samuel Paul, but Sakeem hadn't answered my last question, so I repeated it. "Sakeem, what about the teachings of walk-ins and braid-ins—the question I asked earlier? Why has it been a subject that few discuss?" "Ah, Nakala, simply put, you were not ready to receive this information."

Perplexed and even saddened somewhat, I had wondered why Samuel Paul had stopped his pleasant conversations and valuable teachings. He had stood back, waiting for me to present my questions to him. Now I was beginning to understand.

Sakeem heard my thought and said, "Samuel Paul has a specific post and he will remain focused on that."

On some level I felt like I had lost a long-loved friend. I loved Samuel Paul. Just then I heard Samuel Paul speak. In a very soothing tone, he said, "Nakala, I do not do this out of meanness. It is like I am a support system. I am all around you. Should you tilt a bit, I am here to encourage and aid you in the areas that would benefit you the most—to bring you back to center. In other words, I have your back. I am like a brace for you. This is my function at this time."

CHAPTER
TWENTY-SIX

As it happened, that Sunday morning Father Quem and Mother Sarah were to arrive for our prayers together when a large group showed up as well—The Pleiadian Council of Light. To have others show up is not unusual. However, to have The Pleiadian Council of Light is! I went ahead and welcomed the group, said my prayers and a few affirmations. Then I was directed to get the Pleiadian Council of Light book.

"In Union we come. In greeting we come. We are the Pleiadian Council of Light! We have come to serve you, Nakala."

The books the masters bring you feel have been slow in forth-coming. Perhaps, the energy must come into alignment to bring forth. Know that the finished project is beautiful and perfect in every way!"

"Affirm every day that all is in alignment for the books to be created, edited, published, marketed and sold. There are people who thirst for this type of writing. We quench!"

"All is in motion, Nakala. The energy spirals, shifts always, continuing onward and upward toward higher levels of consciousness—Love and Light.

"Jordan, I speak. (Council Advisor) We watch over many…closely—their order. We assist in ways you know not. It is time you allow additional individual to work with you on the writings.

"Rebeka comes today to work beside you. In this case, she represents the Sirius Council of Light. Rebeka will remain with you as additional guide for the time being.

I asked if this meant Rebeka would be here every day. Rebeka, herself, answered.

"I will be with you every day. Sakeem has gone to work with an individual gentleman. He does have intention to uphold his agreement to assist you with the blog and book! Look for him to continue on this path. It is a sure one. I will be working with you in all areas. Not just the arts.

"Expect Sakeem to arrive every Wednesday morning until he gives further notice.

"Nakala, you are to channel the books—this method of communication. To teach the masses is important—life changing for all.

"I'd like to give you good news. There is buzz—energy stirring that you are to take on another project. This winter there is a person who sees your tenacity and wishes to ask for your hand. I speak of helping hand. Be open to give of your energy.

The next day, as I was directed to add the above transmission to this book, I saw that I had not received it in fullness. I remembered that yesterday, I had suddenly been overcome by exhaustion and had to quit. Now, Jordan wished to finish his message.

"Yes, Nakala, the fatigue you experienced yesterday was a rare occurrence. The frequency was quite high and you were unable to tolerate it for the period required in order to complete.

"The directive has been given that Rebeka guides you. Sakeem stands back. Nathanal will stand back most days, as well. These two are concen-trating their efforts to work with the individual gentleman who will soon join you as companion. They are preparing the way, Nakala. You require a companion to assist you in the physical—to go forward with. Know it is to happen and so it shall!

"The council is quite aware of your progress: what you are working on and the requirement to be fulfilled by the team, Comterous in the future. You are surprised that I direct you to place—disclose— prophetic material in this book concerning a help-mate? Indeed'.

At that point, I lifted my hands in the air, threw my head back and laughed. This is my life with the Beings of Light. They just announce these personal things like it was nothing.

"Nakala, you are the Pleiadian traveler, are you not? You are here for the experience. So it shall come to pass.

"Well now, I have your attention. You are one who will live out your life in extraordinary circumstance! As channel this may be deemed extraordinary in itself as the high percentage of the earth's populace don't believe in this ability, angels, or even spiritual guides (or perhaps it is that they will not admit to believing!) How on earth would they do if they walked in your shoes for a day? For them it would be quite astonishing, I would say.

"Let me continue please…the belief concerning angels is shifting quickly as is the belief in life on other planets (aliens), space crafts, spirit guides and the list grows on from here. We are quite pleased, by the way, to be working with those, such as you, in furthering the cause to enlighten all to possibilities beyond their plausible rationalities.

"We are one of many who are overseeing and guiding the progress of humanity."

It was then that my attention was drawn to the necklace that I was wearing—a double string of cut Labradorite beads of graduating sizes with matching earrings. I had worn them yesterday, for the first time, while the council was here. The implications of this were…I was receiving a frequency that I was not accustomed to. Maybe this is why I felt a little fuzzy-headed.

I wondered how long this Jordan fellow was going to continue his communications with me. On one level, I felt that to teach me or give me information in this book wasn't his area of expertise.

When I acknowledged that I had a headache, someone channeled a breath through me. Then another deliberate breath came through long and deep…and another until Rebeka reminded me, "It is time for you to get lunch."

Throughout Jordan's transmission my phone kept sounding off that it was receiving e-mails of which there were none. Every time my phone had gone off, I had felt obliged to check it since I was selling some furniture. The last time my phone did its thing, Rebeka had said it was time for lunch.

I got up to put some vegetable soup on the stove and said, "Rebeka why don't you just pop the wall or something else instead of making my phone go off?" I heard Rebeka laugh, as she replied, "Because it isn't as much fun!" These guides…I have to just have to laugh sometimes.

Funny, as I sat there I noticed my head beginning to hurt again. I didn't know who was working with me right then. I had become keenly aware that during my entire break my head was fine…

"To answer your question, Nakala, you have a couple of masters working alongside of you—through you who have a high vibration. In addition, you are wearing the labradorite necklace and earrings. You are not yet acclimated to these energies." To clarify I asked, "You are speaking of Jordan and Rebeka, correct?"

"I, Jordan stand on the left side of you, Nakala. Rebeka is to your right and behind you. The labradorite beads are on your person drawing the energies from around you to you. They act as a receiver of sorts. If you wish to lessen the discomfort, remove the necklace." I did as suggested as a test. Just to see what would happen.

The energy immediately shifted and I felt more relaxed.

Jordan said, "I will be staying on a few more minutes…until I have made my mark in fullness." Then Jordan asked, "Tomorrow you are scheduled to write, are you not?"

"Yes. Why?"

"One of the sisters desires to come visit you."

Perplexed I asked, "One of the sisters? Who are you referring to Jordan?"

"One of the priestesses of Telos has been given leave to come work with you for a while." The disclosure left me all tingly, and the emotions I felt were mixed. I felt gratitude for the opportunity, but I also felt a wave of sadness. Probably, the sadness stemmed from the past life I had spent as a Lemurian priestess—a life gone—seemingly taken from me. This might be a trigger for me.

"The one I speak of," Jordan continued, "is one whom you have spent much time with. The reunion will be bitter sweet. In the end the reunion will accomplish much healing, Nakala. Look for her tomorrow." I felt as if I was left hanging with no reference point to her identity; so I asked, "Are you going to tell me her name?"

"No, I shall not disclose this gift. You will understand tomorrow. I must go for now. I have enjoyed my stay with you. Until the next moments, Nakala."

CHAPTER
TWENTY-SEVEN

The forecast—a high pressure system was moving our way, working itself southeast from Alaska. My guides instructed me to move the large potted plants indoors and also any yard art I wanted to winter-over.

Because the pots were over-sized, they were heavier than I could handle. A call to the grounds-keeper had to be made. I really didn't want to—I didn't like asking for help.

Then a little voice said: Putting things off that you could do today never served anyone. While I was thinking about how peaceful my life had become since I began attending to the minute details in my life—by completing tasks and keeping things put away, I remembered this quote from the Master El Morya, "…beauty and order are heaven's first law!"

"Babaró here, Nakala. I'd like to go forward with the teaching if I may. You, Nakala, have always been one to be organized and tidy. However, there is *always* room for improvement. We are guiding you to ease the segments in your day and also balance the mental, emotional, physical and spiritual aspects of you by incorporating and exercising each body throughout every day. You are cognizant of this tactic. The writing exercises the logical-mental, spiritual and emotional. The tasks preformed outdoors and indoors, for the most part, exercise the mental and physical. In short, this is a balancing strategy implemented for you. It would not do at all for you to sit at the computer for long hours channeling our messages. Our aim is to keep you healthy and strong. If we were to encourage you to work for long hours at the computer you would quickly burn-out. We desire greatly to continue our work with you." With that Babaró concluded, "That is enough for today. Tomorrow marks special. Please see that you are rested to receive your guest from Telos."

✳ ✳ ✳

The next morning Babaró didn't push me to get to the computer to begin to write. I wasn't in any hurry either. Finally, there were no more distractions or reasons to put off my writing.

I got myself comfortable at my desk and reread the last chapter, as is my habit, before I write anything new. I was surprised to read about the guest arriving today because I had completely forgotten about her.

Earlier, Babaró had specifically asked me to read his poem, *Evangeline,* that he had written during his last embodiment as Longfellow. I was curious about the poem especially after I had read his biography in Wikipedia. Wikipedia stated that Longfellow had suffered for eighteen years from deep depression after his second wife passed. The depression was debilitating, leaving him unable to write for many years, I questioned Longfellow's sanity, and therefore I questioned what type of poems he really wrote.

So at Babaró's request I had gone to the Mt. Shasta Library to see if they had one of his books I could check out. There I had found the book, *Favorite Poems of Henry Wadsworth Longfellow.* That morning, I had opened the book to *Evangeline* and saw that it was a really a short story written in rhythmic prose. The style was obviously dated.

My question, concerning Longfellow's state of mind and how it had reflected in his writings can never be answered in truth, as his writings were numerous; many published and many most assuredly had not. How was anyone to really get a solid-sure synopsis of another's life unless they themselves somehow were able to magically transpose themselves and live it first-hand? No one really knows the challenges of another. Not really. But I was curious and was willing to give *Evangeline* a chance.

I read two full pages of Evangeline and suddenly, without question, I knew that Longfellow was a gentle man with an open heart. Because of this he was subject to the intrinsic and incredible pain that one may suffer after losing a life companion. For those who have studied Longfellow, remember he had more than his share of loss having two wives and two children pass before him.

All of this reminded me of the years I too had suffered after my eldest son had become irrational and had taken his own life. No longer, though, did I slip away, down deep into the abyss. Now, it all seemed like a distant memory, one that perhaps was grossly imagined—not completely lived.

Babaró announced his desire to begin his dictation. I didn't need any other prompting. I quickly laid down my thoughts of past troubles.

Babaró began by easing in his teaching with, "Our new day has arrived and with it the promise of another season. The temperature has dipped low and the frost has settled on the rooftops. All people, life forms and intelligences sense the shift and prepare themselves accordingly in their own unique way."

Then Babaró shifted his focus on my little mishap last night. "Last eve, you suffered a whimsical downfall. Nakala, you laugh at my choice of words." "Babaró," I sarcastically replied, "not at all, it was more like I snickered."

"You remember who I am, Nakala. I paint the stark-white canvas with words of color to put before my eager audience the scene to evoke the senses." I shook my head and heavily sighed wondering what "color" Babaró was going to use to "paint" what I had done to myself.

Babaró continued his speech with, "Your etheric body was drawn out of your physical body by the dramatic episode of music. As the sounds continued on you went about your business of preparing your meal. With the lyrics and chimes you were taken high—almost completely out of your physical body." There, I cut in.

"Babaró listen, if you are going to tell the story you must begin at the beginning. Instead of allowing him to resume his recollection or his rendition, however, I took over. "This is how it happened. I was going to the kitchen to make Eggplant Parmesan, which takes a good hour. My recipe calls for eggplant, grated carrots, zucchini, an onion, garlic and of course the cheeses. But before I got to the kitchen one of my guides suggested I put on this one CD we really like."

"It had been a full day of writing and I had agreed that, "to loosen up" would be nice. First, I have to explain that Babaró is a fantastic dancer and when a certain piece of music resonates, well…he dances through me like there is no tomorrow. This CD that Babaró had suggested was one we both *really* like! His energy fused with mine and well…it was a load of fun. I knew that would probably happen if I played the CD. I also *knew* that most likely dinner would be delayed because of it.

"Last night, I was particularly hungry and resisted dancing any further than the first two songs. However, I left the music on and headed for the kitchen still rocking with the rhythm. I got my veggies, the cutting board, knives and the grater out and began to prepare the veggies for grating."

Babaró sounded a little put off, maybe even annoyed that I had taken over *his story* and then this time he interrupted me to ask, "Are you finished Nakala?" "Yup, I think so Babaró."

"I speak on this because what occurred was a dangerous marriage. It was all pre-planned on our parts for reasons multifaceted.

"Nakala, you were injured as you grated the carrots on the fanciful hand-held device. Because you had succumbed to the enticing melody of the song, you were not focused on your movements. You watched your movements from a different perspective as you grated the vegetables. A treacherous road you traveled and in one mere moment the deed was done.

"During your night of restless sleep, you brought together—infusing past teachings that applied to this incident. Earlier, I told you that this would be the last major teaching of this book. Indeed it shall be.

"Your etheric body had been expertly and purposefully enticed to expand, drawing it from and out of your physical body as your emotional body also expanded greatly. Your mental body overshadowed by the emotional body in the extreme caused a major imbalance—your emotions had taken over so to speak."

"I put it like this. When partaking in drugs of any kind do the doctors not warn their patients to use extreme caution? This is because drugs or medicines may cause the bodies to become misaligned—unbalanced. The physical body depends on the alignment of all bodies (the divine cosmic matrix) to remain safe at all times.

"Misaligned thoughts—amplified and magnified by emotion—may result in undesirable actions and may cause what you term as accidents. I say there are no accidents just misaligned energy.

"Do you recall when you raked your fingers against the stainless steel cutter? You looked down at them and aloud you asked, "Now what do I do?" You were out of your body and weren't thinking properly. In the barest of description you were unable to think what to do or even feel the pain.

"Babaró, I recall seeing the movements of my hand holding and grating that carrot. I was deep into the music as if under a magic spell and not focused at all on what I was doing."

All at once I questioned why I had not been protected but instead subjected myself to this event and asked, "I wonder where Samuel Paul was during all of this or you, even, for that matter? Aren't you guys supposed to be guiding me for the highest good and protecting me?"

"I remember well you, Babaró, persuaded me to put on that specific CD. Last night just before I put on the CD I had heard part of me whisper, "This isn't the time"…I didn't listen. It all happened so quickly."

This particular CD lends itself to the dance, big-time. It is easy for me to get caught up in the rhythm and go." In an accusing tone, I stated, "Babaró, to put me into harm's way like that was not cool at all."

Babaró channeled a deep breath through me, as I uttered, "Here we go." I knew this was a big lesson. Heck my fingers here were evidence and proof enough.

Babaró started over, "As I said, the incident was preplanned to teach you a few things. The first portion of this message I give to you is extremely important. To stay balanced, you are to be in the body, especially if you are working with objects that are considered a potential risk, like knives and cheese graters. Cars and lawn mowers are ones to remember as well, Nakala."

Inwardly, I moaned as I thought I had a comedian on staff here. "I am real lucky that I can type today. In a way, I was kind of hoping that I might get some time off from this experience."

"Well, Nakala, perhaps you *should* take some time to yourself…lay it down—the writing that is."

"No, Babaró I have tomorrow off. I want to work through this teaching. During the night, I was working to process what happened and for the umpteenth time I was reminded that as a spiritual being I am to stay focused on every thought, emotion and action."

Without prior indication, the image came to mind of Father Quem, specifically, when he had appeared to me in my home. During his visit I had been able to see him with my physical eyes. For hours I had studied his deliberate movements. The way he had carried himself had revealed a man of great authority and wisdom; someone who weighed every option—every single move carefully before he proceeded.

Swiftly and with great force, I was transported in my mind to the time that I had journeyed (with the assistance of Samuel Paul) to the Kingdom of Myra—the city in Pleiades which my father, Quem and mother, Sarah preside over. I saw myself, once again, sitting at the magnificent marble table alongside my Pleiadian family and the members of the Telbar. I saw how those in attendance presented themselves. Those beings were masters and they conducted themselves in that light.

Again, I could see my father respectfully holding the Telbar Book and later the Sirian Council of Light book like they held the secrets of the universe. The care and respect that he took while he handled those books had been incredible and quite palpable. I considered the way he had facilitated the group alongside my mother, Sarah with finesse—a way that seemed effortless. (The meeting took place in Pleiades and had been chronicled in the book, *The Sacred Contract.*)

Intuitively, I could grasp that at some point, I too would shift into that highly expanded state of Being—divinely focused in all endeavors. I realized now that is where I am going—we all are going.

Babaró interrupted my thoughts and called out to me. "Nakala, I am brother to Quem. You are my family. I have come to guide you for the highest good. Sometimes there will be instances that are allowed in order to hit mark, straight-on. Then the teaching is implemented quickly instead of taking months to accomplish. This results in a swift and sure release of unwanted energy to be transmuted into Source energy.

"The corruption of your fingers was not only for you but for humanity. For that incident will bring forth much healing. I bring to the table your

Pleiadian sister, Crystal who presently resides in the physical. You talked to her last eve and told her of your injury. Just saying the words, "cheese grater" caused her to immediately violently react to the point of almost becoming physically ill. Your incident had been a trigger for her and for this reason she too is given the opportunity to benefit from your injury.

"As a healer, Crystal knows the modality to clear the energy of past life trauma. We desired to call her attention to the trauma so she would clear it. This is our gift to Crystal.

"The questions you had concerning how to expand your essence allowing you to take in and to be aware of all that is happening, internally and externally, will be answered in time. When all is in alignment to do so, you will be activated in areas certain, taking you forward, for you to gain expanded consciousness and awareness which result in a higher vibration, a healthier body, and a much longer life span. Of course, there are many other benefits to the expansion of awareness as well.

"Nakala, get up and fix a warm drink for yourself. It is time to shift your focus."

While I was preparing some tea, the name Olim came into the forefront of my mind. Olim was one of a group of four female guides who attended to me when I began to hear my guides speak to me. For some reason the four of them, Olim, Jithury, Colér and Esse all had been in my thoughts lately. It had been years since I last heard from them.

I heard Babaró ask, "Honey, are you ready?" I sighed and answered, "Yes."

"You have a guest who has been waiting to be made known." I stopped typing and waited. No one spoke. I continued to wait and then decided to take matters into my own hands and said, "Welcome." But I didn't know who I was welcoming. I could see a very young woman, small, petite in stature standing near. For a moment, I thought I saw a woman who looked like me. Instantly, I disregarded that vision, instead making my focus on her dress made of violet taffeta. In my mind, I could hear the fabric swish as she moved. The style of the dress was a simple style with a fitted bodice and gathered skirt that came down to her knees. She wore white heals with the tips of the shoes pointed. I saw her dark brown hair styled in an upward sweep with bangs that cascaded over her forehead to the right. She looked like one of those TV actresses straight out of the 60's. Still no one said a word.

Maybe they were talking amongst themselves?

I fidgeted and drank my tea waiting for someone to share with me what was going on. Finally, I heard my name being said, but it sounded far away as if there were a great many miles in between the two of us; our connection just wasn't that great. There, I heard my name again. Still not better. My gaze was directed to the flame of the candle. I closed my eyes, feeling my vibration rise coupled with feelings of love. Tears threatened to spill over. Then someone began to direct me to look around my office at items and words for me to transcribe the meaning or symbolism of—Babaró most likely (his MO).

The word: Shasta

Word: Split

Item: Tape dispenser

Word: Knit

Item: Tape Measurer

Word: Heritage

Word: Control

Item: Numbers on a library book to identify the location

Item: My business card (When Angels Speak) then points to me.

My translation is Shasta is the place I am to mend or glue together or knit (HEAL) the distance or the division with my ancestors (the Lemurians) in a controlled manner or equation (sacred geometry or intention and prayer). It is for me to do.

Suddenly, angry and weary of this way of communication, my voice rose as I declared, "Enough with the games! Who is the woman?" Again, I heard the name Nakala repeated. Listening more closely, I asked again. Again, I heard the name Nakala spoken.

All at once the implications of the clues hit me. The word split used previously caught and held my attention. During that life on the Continent of Lemuria when I sat huddled in that tiny boat with those other women, I had literally split or fractured, leaving behind a soul fragment. It was time for me to retrieve it so I might heal. The woman I saw had been me.

CONCLUSION

During the writing of this book, my brother, David didn't contact me again. I don't dwell on that, but instead am grateful that we were given that time together to heal.

Many teachings have been given to me. With each one I come closer to the full embodiment of love. However, I don't dwell on that either. I am a Pleiadian Traveler and am here for the experience.

PREVIEW THE NEXT BOOK IN

The Accounts of a Pleiadian Traveler

Join Nakala as she travels across the country to assist her Pleiadian sister in caring for her elderly parents after a near fatal accident. There she receives many teachings including one from Timberlund, an ascended master, who shows her that ascended masters disguise themselves in a variety of colors and forms depending on their mission. ~Never are you alone in the scheme of things. ~